SOLDIERS,

HUNTERS,

NOT

COWBOYS

SOLDIERS, HUNTERS, NOT COWBOYS

a Western

AARON TUCKER

Coach House Books, Toronto

first edition

 Canada Council **Conseil des Arts**
for the Arts **du Canada**

 ONTARIO ARTS COUNCIL
CONSEIL DES ARTS DE L'ONTARIO
an Ontario government agency
un organisme du gouvernement de l'Ontario

Canadä

Published with the generous assistance of the Canada Council for the Arts and
the Ontario Arts Council. Coach House Books also acknowledges the support
of the Government of Canada through the Canada Book Fund and the Government of Ontario through the Ontario Book Publishing Tax Credit.

LIBRARY AND ARCHIVES CANADA CATALOGUING IN PUBLICATION

Title: Soldiers, hunters, not cowboys / by Aaron Tucker.
Names: Tucker, Aaron, author.
Identifiers: Canadiana (print) 20220477329 | Canadiana (ebook) 20220477361 |
ISBN 9781552454626 (softcover) | ISBN 9781770567573 (EPUB) | ISBN 9781770567580
(PDF)
Subjects: LCGFT: Novels.
Classification: LCC PS8639.U25 S65 2023 | DDC C813/.6—dc23

FATHERS

'It was like being in bed with Honeyman, when "Thy belly is a sheaf of wheat" led to stories of his father's farm and of her uncle's farm, and the harvesting and threshing.'
— Marian Engel, *The Honeyman Festival*

'Men are created on the principle of destruction. It's like cleansing, ordering, destruction.'
— Stephen Meek (*Meek's Cutoff*, dir. Kelly Reichardt)

SATURDAY

*J*ohn Wayne. I always notice his size first, especially in the opening scene when he gets off his horse and goes to kiss her, Martha, on the forehead. It's a slow kiss. She closes her eyes and grabs his biceps and squeezes. Even though Martha is married to his brother. He bends down to her, from such a height, and kisses her with an incredible amount of tenderness, and she lets her hand linger. Ethan – John Wayne – and his grey cavalry coat. He towers over her. The way he sweeps his hat off his head, despite the wind through the desert. She looks at him after he kisses her, examines his face, smiles, and invites him inside. Like there are no other people in the world, just the two of them.

– Is that how the movie starts?

– No. It actually starts with Martha opening the door to the desert, dust and sand with a scatter of scrubby grass beyond the house's little porch. The background is the giant rock formations of Monument Valley. They're unreal. Small hills sloping, sheer and solid in the middle of the landscape, while things grow and move around them. That's the backdrop for most of the movie. The size of them too. So it starts with Martha, and the camera follows her. We see from her point of view, looking out over the desert from her small house in the middle of all that land. She's in a baby-blue dress. It's Texas in the middle of the nineteenth century, so you can imagine the dress: there is a white apron with a sash wrapped around her waist, tied in a big bow at the back. When the camera cuts to a shot of her, she's pretty, and her lips are so bright. She raises her hand to her eyes to shield them from the sun, to try to see who is approaching. Just as she sees it's him, Ethan, John Wayne, a small figure on horseback approaches, and her husband, his name is Aaron I think, comes up behind her. For a moment her face shows the two men pulling at her from opposite directions, and she's a bit panicked. Then Ethan gets off his horse and walks over and kisses her forehead. For me, the first part of the movie is the secret romance between them. There's another moment later, when she takes off his coat for him and slides it down his arms. And she looks up at him with this quick flirty glance. He totally watches her walk away, admiring her, right in front of his brother. But no one says anything outright in the movie.

– It's a secret?

– It's there. It's just these little moments. But I think it explains parts of the movie later, and why Ethan is as he is. After the kiss, the whole family – Martha, his brother Aaron, their kids – they all go inside their house. The house is adobe brick, with a flat log roof. It is probably the size of this, my apartment. Bit bigger than here, I guess. They all go inside, and Ethan is picking up his youngest niece and talking with her, Debbie. There is Lucy, the oldest daughter, and his nephew Ben. The table is set for a meal, and the dishes are really nice. I always loved the look of that big table set with the blue-and-white dishes, and the red-and-white fabric napkins. My mom had dishes like that, but she would bring them out only on special occasions. Otherwise we ate off these bland beige plates, mismatched glasses. Usually just me and Mom.

– Where was your dad?

– Dad wouldn't be home for most dinners, unless he felt like it, and then there wasn't a lot of warning to make sure things looked nice. But, in the movie, I like how the table is set, with a really elegant teapot with a delicate spout.

– My family always had dinner together. My mother, she worked too but still had dinner ready, and she would always bring all the food to the table and set it up in the centre, and my father and I would sort of attack it. Seeing who could get the best piece of the chicken, or get to the pasta fastest. Like a sword fight, sort of. And my mother, she would watch us – she didn't say much of anything, but she liked having us both at the table. I remember that.

– Our family was so quiet when we were together. It was pretty rare to have us three in one place, and when it happened it was pretty awkward. Until they divorced, when I was thirteen. They both seem much happier now without each other. Anyways, those dishes. The movie came out in the fifties, but I think it gets the Texas pioneer vibe perfectly. Frontier-chic. After, they are all gathered around the table, and Ethan starts giving away his possessions. First, he's got this long sabre. We saw it hanging off him when he walked up out of the desert. It's huge and looks out of place on him. Too decorative. John Wayne, he's menacing, he's violent. In the movie, Ethan, his character, he used to be a Confederate soldier in the Civil War. Him giving it away makes sense, though: he lost the war, he wants to give that away. The Confederacy has failed, he's failed. His whole world view, ideology, failed. His nephew Ben asks him what he's going to do with the sabre and whether he can hold it for a bit. John Wayne just gives it to him.

– You once said I reminded you of him.

– Maybe one of the women at your work told you that.

– They don't even know who John Wayne is. All of them go to university and do the server thing around their classes. I mean it's just some tourist-trap restaurant.

– Plus you're like fifteen years older than most of them.

– Listen, I see the smile on your face. I know you're joking. You liked me enough to date me. That time, I do think about it. We were both bouncing around a bit before going back to school, graduating when we were older.

– I know, I am kidding. A bit. You just get worked up so fast. Anyways, I was thirty-one then, when we were together.

– Right. Almost five years ago now. Yeah, we both had a life before school. And we would go out and you would tell me that you liked that I was older. You spent all day in class around those twenty-year-old boys and you liked being around me. A man. Like John Wayne. Do you remember telling me that?

– I mean, that's true. I did like that about you. But I don't remember saying that. It doesn't sound like something I would say, unless I was very drunk. When was this?

– When we first started dating. You said so one night. In that bar near my old place. I was bartending there. I took you there on one of our first dates and you said I walked like him.

– That was years ago. It was all very intense, and I think we're much better as friends now. You're still a bit intense, but you know, that's you. But no, I don't remember.

– I remember you telling me that you liked that I was doing that restaurant management program.

– I did like that about you too. It seemed like you were on a sturdy path, and I needed some stability. But then, well, we weren't together that long in the end.

– Long enough for me to meet your dad. You said I reminded you of him too. We were at that bar, it's closed now. Everything is closed down now. That place, that stretch along Dundas right near here, all condos, all rich people. They buy condos for their kids. Chinese students, I see them all the time at work, always with full shopping bags.

– Why do you still work there? All you do is complain about it.

– I can't not work, I gotta make money.

– Can you go back to the hotel? That seemed like a good job.

– That job was okay, but the management. And then the other one, yeah, I got, I lost my temper there. So yeah. This job now is easy, bartending still, full-time more or less, and I could move up, if I wanted. But I don't want to be stuck there, managing some place like that. I'd rather just take their money and go home and forget about it.

– But it's full-time?

– Well, they like to move my shifts around sometimes. But yeah, more or less.

– I just can't drink like that anymore. I don't want to, I can't. That's why I suggested here. I can't do the bar thing with you anymore.

– But it's my birthday. Well, almost my birthday. And we do this every year. I would rather be out, yeah, but this is good. I brought myself a birthday present. Us a present. Some of that good bourbon you like.

– Timothy's.

– The bar's name?

– Yeah. Timothy's. You called it Timmy's, like Tim Hortons.

– You don't remember?

– I don't remember much from that time, honestly. I was drinking a lot. Too intense.

– But I reminded you of John Wayne.

– In some ways, yeah. It's all blurred together, that part of my life. You know how it was. I was reckless, I felt out of control. I'm calmer now. Do you want to know about this movie or not?

– I do if it means I can pour us some bourbon.

– I'll have a small one. Very small, but that's it. There's ice in the freezer, help yourself. Put some ice in mine, please.

– Talk loud. I can hear you from here.

– So he is giving away his possessions. He gives a sack of Silver Eagle dollars to Aaron. His brother is scared, like, 'Where did you get these?' He pulls out one of the coins and it doesn't have a scratch on it. They're brand new. He knows his brother, he knows Ethan, and you can see him imagining what John Wayne had to do to get those brand-new coins. So, there's the sabre, the coins. The last thing he gives away to Debbie. She is the youngest, maybe eleven years old. It's after dinner and he's on some sort of rocking chair and his brother is smoking a pipe, in front of this big stone fireplace. Ethan opens his saddlebags in his lap and takes out this really impressive-looking medal. It's got a lovely red-and-green ribbon, and the medal is all gilded, gold with a blue four-armed design. It's beautiful, but also it's like the coins, there is violence in it, an undercurrent. It's dangerous. Martha knows. She says Debbie is too young for it, but Ethan gives it to her anyway. I went down a Wikipedia rabbit hole about the medal. It was actually given to mercenary soldiers from when France was fighting Mexico in the 1860s. So Ethan would have gotten it from Maximilian, an emperor, who led the French for four years, when the French ruled Mexico, then the Mexicans took it back. There is a very famous Manet painting depicting Maximilian's execution by firing squad.

– Do you like the bourbon?

– It's strong. You gave yourself a big pour.

– The only way I make them. Happy birthday to me, cheers.

– Cheers.

– Cheers. So the medal. It's a bit like his fighting for the South. On the losing side again. It's like the sabre too. Ethan is a relic, a failure to the new world being established, and his old things, they don't matter. I mean John Wayne seems proud of the medal when he gives it to Debbie, but, in reality, he got it from fighting on the losing side too. At any rate, he displays it in his giant hand, then he hangs it around Debbie's neck, and she is proud and happy.

– I have a medal from my grandfather like that. I look at it sometimes. I think he got it fighting in the Korean War.

– Well, this medal, I don't know. Maybe Ethan's at a point where objects don't matter to him, or they remind him of lost battles, what he thinks of as better times gone by. Just a bit later in the movie, after everyone goes to bed, he goes out to the porch by himself. And he sits there, looking out sadly at the dark desert. He's lonely, an outcast. A failed mercenary, a Confederate soldier, wandering.

– That's the sort of guy I want to be. No objects, tied to nothing. I don't need things. Just move place to place.

– You want to be like Ethan?

– Yeah, freedom. I really don't like things. Or people telling me what to do. I want freedom.

– I remember your apartment, the one you were in when we met. It was sparse. I used to hate that mattress on the floor.

– That was my first place on my own. I had always lived with roommates, the boys, ever since I came here.

– Do you still talk with them?

– Oh yeah, we're all on a group chat. It's mostly just us sending links back and forth, news and things. Some of the stuff they send is pretty wild, right-wing-type websites. I mean that's just that part of the world, I guess. Do you remember Allan? He's on the group chat, you met him a few times. He just got remarried, though she's … She and I don't get along.

– Allan?

– Tall guy, from out west. He and I came out together originally, drove all the way here. I didn't even mean to stay, but here I am.

– You've moved, I think, three times since we were seeing each other. Remember that one place on Dufferin? With all the junk in the front yard?

– You would come over.

– Once.

– Twice. I liked that place.

– But you really want to be like Ethan?

– The way you describe him, yeah. A cowboy, self-sustaining. My great-grandfather, my father said that he used to run cattle along the lake where I grew up.

– But there is also this other side to him, to Ethan. Throughout the whole film, he is really hateful, racist.

– I mean it was that generation. And then, back in the 1800s, whatever, they were trying to make homes and raise families. Texas, the West. They had to survive.

– But John Wayne. I was listening to a podcast about this movie called *Unspooled*. And they pulled up an interview with him from the seventies with *Playboy*. He says some truly vile things in it.

– But that was his generation. It was different. People didn't know better. And then, back then, 150 years ago, in Texas, what else was he supposed to do? Different generations.

– They named an airport after him.

– After John Wayne? Don't tell me you want it renamed now? They want to rename British Columbia too. Because of Christopher Columbus. I mean, fuck. I just like his attitude. John Wayne's aura. Moving through the world by himself, for himself. Not weighing himself down.

– What other of his movies have you seen?

– *The Shootist*, that is what it's called, yeah? His last one, or one of his last ones. My family, we watched it together after my father's diagnosis, that one and bits and parts of other stuff, on TV or online or whatever. I have seen parts of *True Grit* on YouTube. I mostly just know him as, you know, John Wayne.

– Right.

– The cowboy riding in and shooting people. That scene in *True Grit*. It's amazing. He rides up on this group of four men. He's got an eye patch on. But the best part is when he starts to charge them, one on four, and he holds the horse's reins in his mouth so that he can have both hands free. A gun for each hand. Then he yells something, something like 'Fill your hands, assholes.' So he shoots with the pistol in his left and the rifle in the right, riding fast straight at them, and takes them all out. And there's the one part where he spins the rifle around to reload it, all at full speed. Some *John Wick*–style stuff.

– My dad loves *True Grit*. It used to be on TV a lot late at night. Usually Mom was out if Dad was home, so I would stay up late with him and watch whatever he was watching. So many of the movies were just background, not quite wallpaper, more active than that, but always there. My dad, he didn't care that much which one was on. I just had to run upstairs when I heard Mom come home.

– I had a TV in my room. I would just stay up.

– Mom didn't like me staying up late, especially on school nights. Maybe she just didn't want me sitting with Dad. I don't know. But he always would have some movie on. He didn't drink much, so he might nurse a beer through the whole thing, and I would sit on the couch opposite, watch whatever movie. Truthfully, I don't remember many of the specifics about that version of *True Grit*. You would think I would remember more, especially given Mattie. She's the protagonist. The young woman, the whole movie is her revenge story. I guess I never saw myself in her.

You would think I would identify with her, but no. I think my dad would have liked it more if I were more like her. I'm not sure he knew what to do with me, a daughter.

– My mother told me that if I had been born a girl, they would have just kept having kids until they got a son.

– I don't think Dad wanted a son either, honestly. But he would let me sit near him if I was quiet. Most of the time I wouldn't watch the movie, but watch him. I remember the light from the TV on his face, and his facial reactions to the movies. He still loves Westerns. Every night he was home he would flip channels until he found one.

– My father and I would sometimes watch things together, but mostly sports. He loved baseball, boxing too. He knew a lot about boxing and would get really excited. We would watch fights together, and he would get me up off the couch, replay parts of a round with me. He used to box too. He always told me boxing taught him how to be a man. He set up a heavy bag for me in our basement, and we would go down together sometimes and hit it together. I would hold the bag when it was his turn, and he'd try every time to knock me over. To toughen me up. It was like *Fight Club*. Have you seen *Fight Club*?

– Of course. And read the book.

– It's a perfect movie. But I'm guessing it's pretty different than this one.

– Yes and no. It's not a Western, if that's what you mean, and this one is. But my dad. I don't even really know what Dad likes, aside from Westerns. Gifts are always hard. Birthdays, Father's Days. I often just get him DVDs of the movies we would watch. But he almost always preferred to just watch whatever came on TV, not choose. Even his favourites, the John Ford ones, the John Wayne ones. He would wait until they came on, on their own.

– How many times do you think you've seen this movie?

– Oh, I don't know. Over a dozen, at least as a kid, and at least ten more as an adult. I have a nostalgia for it, or some fascination with it, but I don't love the movie, I mean how could I? It's got racist parts, the Indigenous people are cartoons, played probably by Italians. But I can't shake it. Now I try to watch it at least once a year, usually around my birthday. It's become a ritual, almost meditative, like a way to check in with myself, how I've changed.

– So I should watch it? It's good?

– Maybe, yes. I don't know. I know Scorsese says it's one of his all-time favourites. Spielberg too.

– I like *Goodfellas*. Spielberg, not really, but I loved *Wolf of Wall Street*.

– You know I like movies more than you. Remember I almost minored in film? If you ever want to go back, Scorsese's first film, Harvey Keitel's first film, he talks about this movie in that movie. Keitel, this young, partying, kind of mess of a guy, really misogynist, but he loves the movie. He says something like 'Everyone should like Westerns, the world's problems would be solved if we all liked Westerns.'

– I like the ones with horses and guns and mountains.

– This movie, it's probably the thing, the piece of art, I've thought about the most. That's weird, but it's probably true. One of the few things I know about my granddad was that he also loved the movie. Dad would say that to me: 'You know your granddad loved this movie too.' I think our families, yours and mine, are a lot alike in some ways. I think my great-granddad also had cattle and horses. My dad grew up in the same house where his dad grew up, a farm, pretty big, with lots of space. Maybe thirty acres or more, passed down generation to generation. There's a photo of them I love, him and his dad, and they both look so massive and broad, giant hands, farm boys. Then my parents got divorced. And we never went back, I don't know why. But Dad grew up riding horses as well, mending the fences around the property, that sort of thing.

– We're alike. We're similar.

– In some ways, maybe. We share some parts.

– My father, my family, there were always horses around. There were always lots of fields, but we never had horses of our own. My friends would ride theirs and sometimes I would take one out with them. But that was when I was a teenager, younger. I had such a crush on one of them. Sara. She rode in competitions. She was cute.

– I think you told me about her.

– Yeah, and we got along well, but then once we started going out, I don't know, I lost interest. She would wear this long braid down the middle of her back and would braid the horse's manes sometimes too, in the same way. I always thought that was kind of weird, to try to match her horse. She would let me kiss her, but nothing else, even when I moved her hand, you know?

– I think part of the reason people like the movie so much, why it's so critically revered, is John Ford. That guy was a bit of an asshole too. Mean. Drank a lot. But people, my dad, love his movies, and he did make amazing Westerns. Some of the wide shots he got, especially once he started making movies in colour. Like wow. I do like rewatching them now, on a bigger screen. I would love to see them in theatres, but they are sort of out of fashion. They don't get shown that much because, maybe, the politics of now. On Twitter, someone posted a link to something on Breitbart, do you know that website?

– Yeah, I know it. That group chat, some guys on there post stuff, so I know it.

– It's awful. But they published this article, a long list of the best American movies ever made, or something like that. A lot of Clint Eastwood, those types of movies. And this movie was number one on their list. Let me find it. I want to read something from it. Just a minute, I'll google it.

– I'm glad I brought this. It's very tasty. I don't know why you would put ice in yours though.

– Here it is. Scrolling. Okay, here it is. Okay. 'Ford's theme is that the enormous price paid for what allows us today to enjoy strip malls, coffee shops, carpool lanes, and central air conditioning was paid for in more than just blood by brave settlers, the American Indian, and most certainly the souls of men like Edwards.'

– It was that generation. They had to. It was the wilderness, and someone had to make it so people could live there.

– It's not like they made the movie in the 1850s. The article goes on: the 'justly famous closing scene – still the greatest in all of film – [is] a poignant and wordless reminder that there is no place in civilization for those who made that civilization possible.'

– Civilization. John Wayne, he's an anti-hero. No place. Like, a man who does what needs to be done, even though it's dangerous or maybe not everyone agrees with him.

– He's not an anti-hero like, I don't know, the Joker or Walter White or something. I just don't know what John Wayne even means to most people today. What is he? A dinosaur? Even in the movie itself, he's from a whole other era, a wandering former soldier from two lost wars. He almost always played people from the past, like Ethan, from a century before. He was already playing a version of the past, and now, when we think about him, is that doubled? A past about a past?

– He's iconic. He gets things done, that's what he means.

– All this stuff about the past, MAGA. Always calling to the past. Maybe that is how people think of him now, as from a better past, a better life before.

– Macho. Manly.

– It gets so tangled for me. He is manly. An archetype, for sure. Despite everything, if I'm being honest with myself, it's one I'm sort of attracted to. Maybe I've been trained, through pop culture or something, to be attracted to him. There's the scene, right after Ethan gives away his money, and Martha has to grab the lamp that's high above the fireplace. I mean she doesn't need to, but it's an excuse to be near Ethan. And the lamp is high up, and as she starts to grab it, Ethan reaches up and helps her. It's this small moment, but the two of them take it as an opportunity to hold hands, steal a look at each other. He does love her in a way that is both fierce and restrained. She longs for him, he pines for her, but she's his brother's wife. Still, he's bold and handsome, and he makes sure she knows how he feels, in his way. That side of John Wayne.

– And the other side?

– The other side is cruel and aggrieved. Furious. And he always thinks he has valid reasons to be that way. That there is always justification for his anger, a righteousness. The movie argues that the world made him a certain way, forced him into being a soldier, into fighting a failed war, then blamed him for fighting. It's not his fault, it's never his fault. In fact, it's heroic to be that way. The next day the sheriff rides up to the cabin and explains that someone stole some cattle from a nearby home. They have their trail but they need help. So would Ethan and Mart be willing? I'm not sure why, no one gives a reason, but Ethan's brother stays with his family, which ends up being important. Ethan and Mart go.

– Mart?

– The young guy. His family was killed, and Aaron and Martha rasied him. He tries to call Ethan his uncle and Ethan loses it, tells him never to call him that. Mart is not his family. That's the side I'm talking about. Ethan's a principled person. He believes in family and that sets up the plot of the movie. But that same protective energy just as easily turns into an isolating force, Us vs. Them. And so he draws fast conclusions around his very rigid principles, no compromises. The very fact that the world has changed and demands changes of him infuriates him. They all ride out to get the cow thieves and it's beautiful. Ford really was an incredible director, if only for his shots of Monument Valley. It's all about scale, so vast. The mountains look so giant and the desert goes on forever. There is this one shot, with those massive rocks, and they are catching the light, a rusty colour, and the sand is gleaming, and the shot is from far away so you almost don't see the group of riders, you really only see their dust. And they are tiny. So small against the rest of the shot. It's stunning.

– I would love to go there. It sounds incredible, like parts of BC, around where I grew up.

– It's hard to even understand that it is real, Monument Valley, that it is a place you can go. The colours, you just can't see them anywhere else. The hues of purple that creep into the shadows. The landscape, it looks earthly, but with a slight warp to it. Unreal, resized, rescaled, frightening, massive. Yet there is also the flat line of the horizon that holds it steady, gives it a sense of the normal. It's all mixed together. So, they come across the cattle and see these long lances buried in the sides of them. John Wayne pulls one out and tells them that they're from Comanche. He holds it in his hands and the sharp head of it glistens. He looks natural holding this weapon, with his leg up on the dead cow. He's got on a red shirt and has a blue handkerchief around his neck, maybe for the riding dust, chaps and hat. He's angry, really angry. He realizes it's a decoy, that the Comanche are on a murder raid. They only wanted to get everyone away from his brother's house so they could attack it. Everyone wants to rush off, especially Mart. But Ethan doesn't move. He explains they have to feed and water the horses before they go, otherwise they'll, the horses, will die underneath them as they ride. He's furious, you can see it boiling inside him. But he's also this calm presence, like a predator, that knows the land, knows the horses, he knows everything. Mart rides off without him and, sure enough, the next time we see him, Mart's walking with his saddle. His horse died somewhere underneath him along the way.

– John Wayne is smart then.

– Ethan is the smartest person in the movie. That's a part of what makes him that much more seductive. But it's his anger that drives him, is core, fundamental to his being. That core, I don't think it's uncommon. I see it in other people too, other men.

– Me?

– At times, yes.

– I'm kind.

– You can be, yes.

– I just don't put up with stuff. But I don't see myself as an angry person.

– There was that week you took care of me. After my surgery, and you came over every day and looked after me. Made me dinner and watched TV with me. I was thinking about that when you texted and I invited you over here.

– But even after that, and I took care of you, you still think I'm, like, I have this other side?

– Just, let me. Mart comes over the ridge that looks down on the home and it's in ruins. The smoke is pouring out of it, the stable is also on fire. The smoke, clouds of it, black with flames dancing underneath it. He thinks they're all dead, Aaron, Martha, the entire family. He doesn't know it yet, but Lucy and Debbie have been kidnapped and everyone else was killed. He rips his rifle from the holster and sprints his horse toward the wreckage. And he shouts her name. 'Martha! Martha!' And he pulls out a charred dress smudged with dirt too. It looks like it's been ripped off her. Then he finds her body. We don't see it, but we do see him slump when he finds it. He looks small, broken. But that moment is also where it begins, the angry engine of the movie. His vengeance, his grief. She's another thing he's lost. I think the whole movie is about that grief.

– He has to avenge her.

– Yes and no. And this is where you can understand his motivations, like I was saying before. He comes upon this massacre, his dead brother, and maybe the person he loved most in the world. Maybe the only person. And he's furious, but he needs to direct that fury somewhere. He's hell-bent on revenge, yes, on repaying that violence. You can understand why he would feel that way. After you understand it, then you have an easier time allowing everything else that follows. It's justified. That anger and hate.

– I would do the same thing.

– But there's that other side again. His anger, his grief, justifies everything he does in response.

– What else was he supposed to do?

– I don't know. I understand it on some emotional level, but I don't agree with it.

– I don't know what else he could do. Someone murdered his whole family.

– I think that's what makes me afraid. It's less about that and more about how the anger mutates from inside a story, a movie, out into the real world.

– Revenge.

– It's not just his revenge, though. The movie is not that simple. Earlier in the movie, we get to see his brother's home just before it gets attacked. They know the war party is coming, and we see Aaron push Debbie, the younger niece, out of the window. He tells her to go hide in the cemetery. But she's found right away by the main villain of the movie. Scar. He's the chief, and he is shirtless, brightly painted, with a war headdress. It's nearly every terrible stereotype you can think of.

– But that's how they were back then. I grew up around them. We had a family across the street, and I would always drive past the reservations. I went to school with them. Native. Indigenous. That is how Indigenous people were back then, like in the movie.

– That is what the movie would have you believe. It's not true. But that's how they are portrayed in the movie: they're predatory animals, very scary. So, they kidnap Debbie and Lucy and kill the rest.

– I've read about Texas and New Mexico at that time. I read this really interesting biography of Kit Carson that talks about how that part of the world was a mix of the Spanish, from Mexico, and the various Indians, mostly the Navajo, and then white people from the Northeast. The book explains that that was how the tribes were. They were ruthless, and if you didn't fight back, or even fight first, you'd just die. You had to be pre-emptive. Kit Carson, that guy had a wild life.

– I don't know much about him.

– You should read this book. He basically established the West. He had a bunch of wives, some of them were Natives. He went out and conquered the West. But the Natives he cleared out, that seemed like a really rough battle, even though he respected them. But it had to be done.

– You would like this movie then. There is a lot of that in it, and it's one of the things that pushes Ethan forward. He is on the hunt for Debbie and her sister. All of this happens in the first twenty minutes, and the rest of the movie is John Wayne hunting for them.

– I think my father would have liked this movie.

– I know maybe it's hard to talk about, but does the movie, the way I'm describing it, does it remind you of him?

– He did die around my birthday, close anyways, so I have been thinking of him.

– I'm sorry.

– No, it's okay. I've told you when we've talked about him in the past, I was more or less an adult when he died. Seventeen. Well, almost seventeen. He lived his own way and didn't really look after himself that well. And then it was on top of him. The day he collapsed. In the fucking mall, if you can believe it. He was alive for a few more days, so I spent time with him at the end. He got his diagnosis and then really stopped taking care of himself. I mean he would still eat and dress. He wasn't depressed. He was really strong, all the way to the end. But he just stopped doing what the doctors said. My mother would tell him he was killing himself, but he said he wanted to go out on his terms. I know I've told you all this before, I'm just thinking of it again right now.

– It's okay. That must have been hard.

– *The Shootist*, we did watch that maybe a couple months before he died. I do remember him saying once that John Wayne was his kind of guy. A man's man. He beat cancer, and after my father was diagnosed, that suddenly meant a lot more. My father. It was probably harder on my mother. I think that was why I left. I did that one year at community college after he died, and that summer Allan and I drove out here and I dropped out. I didn't think I would stay, I just needed to get away. I miss it there, I miss the landscape and the valley and the ranchland. I think about it a lot. My father though, I'm okay now. But sometimes I'll see a movie, or read something, or get into a conversation with someone, and something will flash, it'll remind me of him. He probably would have liked this movie.

– It's such a strange movie in some ways. For me, it all starts with Martha and Ethan. This unspoken romance, desire. For me, their relationship, I guess non-relationship, it helps me understand Ethan's motivations. Why he is so relentless.

– My mother used to call my father that, *relentless*. She yelled it one time.

– We don't have to talk about him.

– No, I'm drinking. That's the only time I think about him. It's okay. But tell me more about the movie.

– Okay. I'm sorry. The movie. Next there's a funeral, for Martha and Aaron, but John Wayne just wants to leave. I have thought a lot about his grief in that moment. Most of it is for Martha, if not all of it. He doesn't mention his own brother, the movie doesn't linger on him, it's all Martha. And the ritual of the funeral is worthless, the civilized way of laying Martha to rest. He wants to remember her by exacting a terrible but proportional violence. His vengeance. He just wants to get on his horse and get his justice. To make it right in that way.

– I don't think I cried at my father's funeral either. It's not like I was happy he was dead. Nothing like that. But I didn't feel like crying. I just didn't. But I watched everyone and I made lists. Lists of things I could do, lists of people who brought things, who made phone calls. Who helped my mother. I remember I actually made a list of people who cried.

– Grief does things.

– I never told anyone that before.

– It's okay.

– I think you bring it out of me. I've always liked that.

– It's okay to grieve, even still.

– I do remember wanting to really hurt someone. The paramedics. They could have saved him. Or should have. My mother kept telling me to stop yelling. I was yelling a lot then. All the time.

– I think it's natural to feel anger. Though, sometimes, when we were together, if I'm being honest, it would scare me.

– But not now. I'm fine now. Anyways. I want to hear more, about the movie I mean.

– I can if you're okay?

– I'm fine.

– Good, okay. After the funeral, a group of men ride off and you really get a sense of how well John Wayne could handle a horse on film. There is something so natural about him on horseback. He belongs to the world of the movie in a way no one else does. You really see it best when they are riding through this vastness, with mountains and sky. They are riding and then they come across a fresh grave. It's a warrior, one that his brother was able to kill before he died. The other men are afraid because they know that the only reason the Comanche wouldn't bury their dead was if they were running. They think the grave means an ambush.

– Do you want another drink? I'm getting another.

– Okay, last one. A small one again, with ice please. Thank you.

– Keep talking.

– The movie, it's gruesome. One of the guys snaps and starts to bash the corpse with a rock until the sheriff stops him. But John Wayne, he's still on his horse, and he says something like 'Why don't you finish the job?' and shoots the dead body. Twice.

– Whoa.

– It's intense.

– Yeah, no, that too. But I was also looking out the window, in your kitchen. There's a couple on the street and she's really yelling at him. Like really yelling, and he looks pissed.

– It is Saturday night. Stuff happens, people are out. And it is getting late.

– It's only ten.

– Late for me.

– Whatever it is, they were really yelling. Anyways, here's yours. Cheers.

– Thanks. Cheers. Happy birthday again.

– I saw beer bottles next to the fridge. You don't drink beer, do you?

– They might be left over from someone else.

– Oh, I bet it's that Phillip guy. Was it him? He's so arrogant.

– I know he bugs you.

– Does he come over a lot?

– We're just friends. We don't need to talk about him.

– Have you told him about this movie?

– No, I don't think so. It's not something I usually talk about.

– Good, he's never heard you talk about this movie. I definitely want to know what happens now.

– Ah, well, yes, after they find the dead body, John Wayne explains that he shot his eyes out because they believe that if any of their body is missing when they die, then that spirit is doomed to wander the afterlife forever. And in this case blind. The men are supposed to be following the sheriff, but it's obvious that Wayne is in charge. And he's so magnetic, he really is, throughout the film. But I think it shows how cruel he is.

– Because he shot a dead guy?

– Because he doomed this other person. You have to remember, too, they are looking for the two young girls, to see if they're alive and to rescue them. That's what they are supposed to be doing. But he stops long enough to shoot a dead man. He's vindictive, spiteful. He's just buried Martha. Do I think Ethan loved Martha? Yes. And she, in her way, loved him in return. But the reality was that neither of them did anything about it. Maybe they couldn't, or didn't feel it was even possible. I wonder sometimes. I know lots of men who like women they know they can't get involved with. There's a safety in that, a way to guard against getting hurt or being vulnerable. I think Ethan loves Martha more once she is dead. That her death, and whatever feelings he had for her, unlock a new level of anger and hate and cruelty for him. At that point, for most of the movie, I don't think it matters much what Martha thought or felt. Her death allows him the freedom to be how he really is.

– You think all this because he shot a dead guy?

– Because he shot him in such a way that his spirit would be trapped, unhappy, forever. Isn't that messed up?

– I suppose.

– The other people want to get the girls back. That's their priority. So they go off and they finally catch up to the group, to the Comanche war party, and they are discussing how to approach them and get the girls back. Ethan wants to charge them, but the sheriff makes the point that if they do that, they run the risk of the war party just killing their hostages, the girls. The better way would be to approach them on foot and not escalate things right away. But that's not what Ethan wants. He wants to kill as many of them as possible. But he's talked out of it, and they do sneak up. The scene is really striking: they wade through this swamp, on foot, and the mist is coming off the water as they approach, they look like ghosts creeping forward. The light is really pretty too. It's dusk, in between, a limbo, especially with the mist, that is really memorable. The best parts of the movie are a bit unearthly like that. They get to the place where the war party had had a fire, but they are gone. They got away. Ethan was right, of course. Hold on, there's a book I want to get. I was just thinking of it, as I remember that scene.

– You have so many books.

– I find them comforting.

– Were we ever like that?

– Like what?

– Like that couple fighting out on the street. They were really in each other's faces. He was coming right at her. I mean he was in her face. They were under the street light at the corner, by the door to your building. You said I scared you, a side of me, was I ever like that?

– You would get some angry sometimes, at other things. A guy riding his bike on the sidewalk, or someone playing music without headphones. I always felt like you acted one way to me, but underneath you felt a whole other way. Angry, like I said. Like you knew what you thought I wanted to hear, but I'm not sure you believed it as you were saying it. You know how to act. But toward me, I mean, we did have that one fight. You accused me of thinking I was too smart for you. But us, dating, it was so brief. How long was it?

– It was four. It was a good four months. Plus, you know, after, even now. I liked us together. We got along. Do you remember that party? The first time? I still think about it a lot. You were wearing that bright yellow dress that is sort of lacy.

– Dandelion.

– What?

– It was dandelion.

– Okay, sure. And we kept making eyes at each other. I had seen you at the bar a few times and I would think about you for the rest of the shift, the next day. I wanted to get to know you. Then you were at that party.

– You did come right over. You said hello. Shook my hand. A gentleman.

– I was raised right. Making out, just outside your apartment. We were good together. We went to the island that one day. That was fun. But Phillip?

– He's just a friend.

– Whatever, it's my birthday. What happens next? Tell me.

– Okay, okay. It's actually one of the more exciting parts of the movie. John Wayne and the men with him, they are riding along in a line, and there is a hill behind them. One scout from the war party gets to the top of the hill, over its crest, and looks at them. There is a fair bit of distance between the group and the scout, so they can't shoot at him. He's bare-chested and painted, feathers in his hair, the whole thing. The horse he is on is so beautiful. Chestnut. And he waves his arm back over the hill, where we can't see, like 'Come on,' and the rest of the war party shows up. And Scar is there. And I didn't notice it the first few times, but when they show him, you can see the medal that

Ethan gave Debbie hanging around his neck. Everyone has their guns out, measuring each other. And there is this one shot, it's framed so beautifully, with John Wayne's group at the bottom of the frame riding single file, then Scar's above them on the hill, and you can see that group in profile. They are mirrors of each other, shadows of each other.

– Why don't they just shoot each other?

– They're waiting. Soon we see that there are actually two war parties, one on each side, and Ethan's group is in this little valley between them, surrounded. So Ethan and his men, they bolt, right at the camera. It's loud, and you can really see the horses move. You can see the men and their horses with their necks down, running really hard. The war parties join up into one big group and start chasing them. There is dust everywhere, and John Wayne's group is ahead and makes it to this wide river first. They are rushing across with their horses, and you can see them slow down a bit as the horses start swimming. The war party tries following, but their horses spook or something, they can't get across, and the horses fall over, bucking the men off their backs. Ethan's group makes the other side, sets up behind some logs. One of them got hurt, but everyone else is okay, and they wait for the war party to try charging across the river. It's a standoff. John Wayne's group holds them off, turns them back. They retreat, but Ethan is still shooting at them, yelling. He doesn't stop. After, Ethan and his men, the group, decide that it would be easier for a smaller group, one or two, to find the girls. Of course Ethan says he's going to go alone, but Mart insists on coming too, and this other young guy, I can't remember his name. The three ride off, back across the river. The water is up to the horses' necks, the banks have this really pretty red in them.

– My father, I was just thinking about him as you were talking. I sort of zoned out, but I'm listening. Why did your dad like this movie so much?

– I think about that a lot. He liked you. He told me after we broke up. I think you two are the same, made in similar ways. But my dad and I, we don't talk much anymore. I just can't. It's hard to pinpoint the exact reasons. Nothing traumatic, no blow-up. I just can't.

– And I'm like him?

– Do you want to know the rest? Of the movie?

– Yeah. Sure. Tell me.

– Okay. It's just the three of them, and they are following the war party's trail when it suddenly splits. Ethan tells them each to take a different path and loop back together afterward. So they do, and John Wayne is the last one to come back. He rides back all crazy – he comes over the mountain almost in a panic. He gets off his horse. More like stumbles. It's the only time in the movie where John Wayne doesn't seem in control. He stumbles into the sand, sits down, and starts drinking from the canteen without saying anything. The other two, they keep asking him what's wrong and he says nothing. It's the part of the movie that makes it clear that John Wayne could act. But when you put him next to the other actors in the movie, he is so modern. Everyone else, they have these big gestures, screams, shouts, exaggerated emotions. Mart especially. Very handsome, but not a good actor. John Wayne, though, in this movie especially, he could be in a movie today, right now, and he would fit in. I think he understood the movie screen, how any small thing becomes magnified, and so his sort of stoicism plays really well. He's subdued, restrained. He's really good in this movie.

– Did he ever win an Oscar?

– For *True Grit*. But this movie is the height of his fame. Even though he's a bit older, he's still imposing. That's what makes the scene so jarring, that he is panicked. He doesn't explain why at first, then eventually calms down. The three continue on, and there is this gorgeous part, the three are close to the camera, but behind them it stretches out flat forever. That's the thing about the movie: Ford makes it seem like they are, the characters of the movie, they are the only humans in the world. Everything else is untouched. The landscape is dramatic, desert, but the giant rocks are off to the side and it's just an ocean of sand all the way to the horizon. Everything else has been eradicated. And the three are the only people left in the world, riding their horses.

– It sounds a bit like near where I grew up. In the early nineties, when I was younger, the ranch near me, it was owned by some British businessmen, and they did everything on the ranch with technology. Then a new owner bought the ranch, and they went back to the old ways, with cowboys and cattle. I would drive by with my family, look out the window, and see the men riding horses as the sun went down.

– Like you were living in a movie.

– Real-life cowboys.

– In the movie, they aren't really cowboys. Soldiers, hunters, not cowboys. At this point in the movie, there's the three of them: Ethan, Mart, and the third guy, I can't remember his name, I always forget it. But he's in love with Lucy, Debbie's older sister, and is there to get her back. Eventually they do catch up to the war party and this third guy runs up to them and says he's seen them. Actually, he says he saw Lucy wearing a dress he recognizes, and she's there with the war party up ahead. Right away Ethan says it's not her. It can't be her. And the other two, they are confused. 'It's her, I saw her,' he says, and again Ethan says no. 'Why not?' So he tells them it was a man in her dress, trying to trick them. They don't believe him. 'How can you be so sure?' 'Because I buried her,' he tells them.

– So the war party killed her.

– Yes. He says that he found Lucy's body back in the canyon. When the three split up. That's why he was so panicked when he came back. He tells them he wrapped her up in his coat and dug the grave with his hands. Picture that, him clawing at the earth, trying to make a grave for her, wrapped in his clothes. They raped her, left her body in the desert, and took her dress to wear.

– Fuck.

– Martha is dead, and her oldest daughter has been raped and murdered, and Debbie is still out there, and suddenly Ethan's furious, beyond furious. He's been keeping all that inside, to protect the other two maybe, or maybe because he couldn't say it and confront it. So it morphed into rage.

– That's how life was back then, though.

– The movie isn't a documentary.

– I get that. But at the same time, that was actually how life was. That Kit Carson book.

– The movie presents it all as fact too. But it's not a fact. It is an argument the movie is making. I'm talking about a certain type of masculinity that presents itself as fact.

– But that's how it was. I know you're on Twitter and whatever and maybe you think all this stuff about toxic masculinity, but I don't know how else they could have been back then.

– At any rate, the third guy, who loved Lucy, he loses it. He runs away from Mart and Ethan, he gets on his horse and he rides right into the war party. Basically commits suicide. We don't see it because it happens off-screen. But we see Mart and Ethan's reactions to the gunshots. Each character has different forms of grief. How it manifests in each of them. I think we are supposed to side most with Mart. Maybe his grief is the most recognizable, the safest. He is upset that his adopted mom and dad and brother have died, and that Lucy and Debbie were kidnapped and want to rescue them. He's almost there to offset Ethan, and his fury. But John Wayne is John Wayne, and it's impossible not to side with him. To see things from his perspective. And he's transformed. I mean you get the sense that Ethan was always angry, but now it combines with grief and violence.

– It makes sense to me.

– How?

– I grew up with a kid, went to elementary school with him. This guy, Joel, he was the biggest liar I knew. He would make up the craziest stories, just insane. There was one, he told me he had had his head cut off, and he was carrying it around and he could still talk and everything. He would tell stories like that, and he lied about everything. It was mostly sad. I don't know why he did it. No one ever believed him and we all made fun of him. Our school wasn't that big, a couple hundred kids for all seven grades. Everyone knew him, and everyone knew he was this giant liar.

– That's kind of sad.

– At any rate, his family had a pool, and I guess it wasn't fenced in or anything. One day his younger sister falls in, and she gets tangled in the pool covering, and she drowns. I think she was like six or something.

– Oh my god.

– And after that, he got to do whatever he wanted. At least until they moved. He didn't come back to school for a while, obviously, but when he did he would draw on his desk these sort of dragon-type creatures, in pen, and the teachers would just let him be. He wouldn't hit people, but he definitely got more angry at, like, baseball, when he struck out or whatever. I was maybe nine when this happened.

– That's awful.

– It was pretty fucked up. So the family ended up moving and I forgot about him. Everyone else was playing hockey and travelling all over the province, but I didn't really like it. I couldn't skate that well. I did karate for a bit. And I played softball. I liked sports but for whatever reason couldn't quite find what I wanted to get into. But then I started bowling, maybe in Grade 6. I wasn't bad at it. I mean I wasn't super good at it either, but I was one of the better people in our league. We would drive into town once a week and do the league thing and sometimes we would travel for a tournament. But Joel ended up on my team. He was better than I was, way better. And we ended up getting to know each other again. Turns out his mom and dad split up not too long after they moved. But he was at a school he liked and was feeling better. We never talked about his sister and the drowning, or how he used to lie about everything. We weren't that close, but we were friends. He was way more mellow, and just happy.

– That's nice.

– I'm almost done this bourbon.

– I don't need another, thanks.

– It's my night off. They gave me the weekend off. Am I going home after? You're not done the movie. You sure you don't want another?

– Yes, positive. Just keep talking from the kitchen.

– Okay. Sure. So one weekend we were all going out of town, maybe Cranbrook or someplace like that, for a bowling tournament. We were staying overnight, wherever it was. And Joel was coming, there was a team of eight or so of us, and my parents were driving up in the truck like always. They usually drove and we would often take other kids with us. So we're going to Cranbrook or wherever and Joel's not there to be picked up. We don't even go by his house. My parents don't really explain, we just leave. My mother and father were not the most open people. My father especially. This weekend they were quiet. My mother would usually at least point at things as we drove and make comments. But that weekend they were extra quiet, and they didn't bring Joel up once. And I noticed that they didn't have the radio on either. My father loved listening to the radio, just having the noise in the truck, I think, and so it was always on. But, nothing. I did the whole tournament thing – I can't remember much about it specifically. But as we're driving back, my mother, she turns to me and, very quietly, she explains why Joel wasn't there. The Friday, the day before we left, his father showed up at his mother's house. Some of this I learned from the papers, after. His dad shows up, murders her and her new boyfriend and then kills himself. It was insane. I don't think I saw Joel again after that. It happened a lot where I grew up, when I think about it. It was always kind of a dangerous place, even though it was small and seemed pretty cozy from the outside. Even now, when I tell people I'm from the Okanagan, the first thing they say is how pretty it is. But there were bikers that would drive up and down the valley. They sold a lot of coke, there was a lot of coke around. Even now, lots of pills, opioids. I knew kids in high school who dealt. One of them had a police officer for a dad. There was always lots of petty shit. Break-ins. Stealing. Stealing and drugs. But also, do you remember the Gakhals?

– Maybe. Sounds familiar.

– It happened a few years after the Joel thing, maybe two or three. It was this family across town. There was actually quite a big Sikh population there, but they all went to the other high school. But they were the only non-white people in the area. I'm exaggerating, but not really. Where I grew up was very white. And very conservative.

– I remember some of what you told me. It seemed pretty small.

– It's a bit over thirty thousand people. But super high crime rate, drug rate. Anyways, the Gakhals. There was a big wedding one weekend, giant wedding for the family. Like three hundred people. There was an ex-husband, I think the sister was getting married. He drove down from the coast, probably a five-hour drive. Got to their house while they were all preparing for the wedding, and he went into the house and just started shooting people. He killed nine people and then left. He went back to his hotel and shot himself. Nine people in this small town.

– And this was normal?

– No, not normal, no. Looking back at it now, yeah, it seems strange. Just a small little place. The tourists would come through every summer, stay at the lakes and fish or boat around. Maybe. I think I thought it was normal. How could I have known?

– No, it's true. Do you think it affected you?

– What do you mean?

– All that: the Gakhals, your friend's dad, these ex-husbands. I don't see how you breathe it in every day and not be changed by it. I don't mean it as an insult. I'm just thinking.

– No. Nothing happened to me. I mean I guess my father dying, but I was old enough to handle it eventually. I honestly don't think about any of it very often. It just was how the world was, how it happened. Evil exists everywhere. Violence. It happens everywhere. It happens here, in Toronto.

– It's true. But I'm not sure it's evil. Evil is something else entirely. Yes, okay, the stories you just told me, really dramatic examples. But I'm thinking about something more systemic. Violent, furious people. Men. That's not evil to me.

– I turned out fine. I don't think it changed me in any real way. Sometimes people do evil things. It did scare my father, though. Well, he never said he was afraid, but he changed. He started shooting his guns more. And he got me a gun and taught me how to shoot.

– You had a gun?

– I still do, yeah. I have a licence for it. I had to do the two-day safety thing.

– In your apartment?

– Yes, in my apartment. I haven't taken it out since I moved in. But my father insisted I learn and keep it with me. He gave it to me about a year before he died.

– You have a gun in your apartment?

– A handgun, yes. It's not a big deal.

– It is a big deal!

– This is why I kept it to myself. I knew you would freak out.

– I am freaked out!

– Didn't your dad shoot?

– You have a gun.

– It's not a big deal. I'm very safe. And I never take it out. It's not even loaded right now. It's just to have. For security.

– Security against what?

– Just peace of mind, I guess. My father gave it to me. It's like a memento. After the Gakhal family, and after the Joel thing, he insisted. He told me that he didn't know when things were going to go crazy, and I needed to be able to defend myself. Just in case. It's been years since I've shot it, honestly. Just after he died. I went up to the spot in the forest where he first taught me, and I shot at some beer bottles. My father hunted, and his father hunted, and there were always guns around. Mostly rifles. But the first handgun I saw was after the Gakhals. And then he bought one for me too. There was a lake that we used to go fishing at when I was younger. Back then we would take the little boat out and row and then cast some lines and wait. But after those shootings, we would go up to that lake and do target practice. I was better at it than I was at bowling. I was a good shot, actually.

– How did I not know this about you? Fuck.

– It's fine. Trust me.

– I am not coming over again until it's gone. I never want to see it. Promise me.

– I promise.

– Okay.

– What happened next? In the movie?

– Changing the topic?

– Yes. Changing topics. Distracting you. Whatever. Tell me what happened after the third guy dies and it's just the two of them.

– John Wayne, Ethan. And Mart.

– And?

– They keep looking for Debbie, for the little girl. They don't know if she's alive or not. Ethan suspects, because she's so young, they wouldn't just kill her. That they might try to raise her until she's old enough to be married, have kids. Ethan is so angry at even that thought.

– So they keep looking for her?

– I'm sorry, I can't get over the gun.

– Please just keep going. It's not a big deal.

– And it was there when we were dating.

– Yes, but I didn't ever take it out. It's just for safety. I'm safe. Please, the movie.

– I don't know. Okay. I just. Okay. Okay. They get desperate. The movie skips ahead in time, and they are in the snow. Seasons have gone by. They ride, slow, over a frozen lake, or it looks like a frozen lake, and the flakes are coming down, coating them and their horses. John Wayne has on dark clothes, and he's filthy with all the riding. It is such a contrast: him tall and dirty on his horse and then the snow around him, glaring white. They talk and agree they have to go back, back to his brother's old house to get more supplies, try to learn more about where she might be, and try again. I can skip the next part of the movie. It is a bit boring.

– Boring how?

– It's slow and almost tangential. They get home and there is a letter waiting there for Ethan. And in it is a scrap of a dress that a trader bought, and Ethan thinks it's a part of Debbie's dress. They leave again. They get directions from the trader, a new lead on where Debbie could be, but the trader double-crosses them and tries to kill them. There's a gunfight and John Wayne kills everyone. Mart accidentally trades some coffee or something for a wife.

– That doesn't sound boring at all. A gunfight!

– Yes, but the part with Mart's 'wife.' Basically he thinks he's getting a hat from this tribe they come across, but it turns out he traded for a wife. So she starts following them. She's basically a slave, and Mart keeps getting more and more frustrated with her. At one point Mart ends up kicking her down a hill. It's all played for laughs. I don't know what it's doing in the movie. It doesn't add anything to the plot other than they ask her if she knows Scar and she gets really scared and eventually runs away.

– It was like that back then too. Kit Carson, he had a few wives from different tribes. It was pretty common.

– Anyways. I don't like this part of the movie. It's like fifteen minutes or so. It's dull and racist.

– But you still watch it.

– I still do, yes. It's part of the ritual. But maybe I'll check my phone or go make tea during that part.

– You wouldn't fast-forward?

– No. That would feel like cheating. Sometimes I wish I had a version of the movie I had taped off the TV, with commercials, like I used to watch.

– Why?

– I don't know. It wasn't like watching it with Dad, late at night, is a good memory. It's weird. It is just the version of the movie that is in my head. The part just before Mart and his wife, it has one of the movie's more famous lines. It's winter, and Mart and Ethan lose all the trails. The snow is covering up everything and they concede that they have to go back. And Ethan has to explain that he isn't giving up. It's one of the famous parts of the movie, where he explains that a Comanche will run until he thinks whatever is chasing him has stopped. But John Wayne, he says, 'There is such a thing as a critter that just keeps coming. Just as the turning of the earth,' and that they've never seen anything like him before. At this point in the movie, I think it's the only thing he knows. It's his nature. His relentlessness. It's as natural as the world turning and the sun rising and setting every day.

– He's got principles. He won't stop.

– Maybe, in some ways, I guess. It makes how he is seem natural, like maybe he's a force of nature. His vengeance, he's like the earth turning. But he's not just hunting revenge. We do get both sides of him. I just come back to him and Martha. The movie is never overt about them. The closest we get is back near the start of the movie, before Martha and his brother are killed, there is a small scene, just Ethan and Martha. She hands him his riding clothes, his army uniform, folded neatly with care. And she hands it to him like she's handing him his armour, and he takes it, and they never break eye contact. They don't say anything, but it's there. She watches him ride off, and her dress is the same colour as the sky, and the ribbon around her waist is the same colour as the clouds.

– He's a good man. A man of principles. But that is how people are, though. They have multiple sides.

– The core tragedy of the story is that he is someone who doesn't belong anywhere, John Wayne, Ethan. He is too savage. He's actually more like Scar than anyone. He fought for the South and lost, that whole ideology lost. He doesn't fit in with this frontier life gaining ground, setting up farms and churches and trying to 'civilize' the space. He knows all this, I think, and that's why he gives away all his things at the start of the film. He has no use for them because he's not of that world. He doesn't need an ornamental sword, he doesn't need a medal or money. He just needs his horse and his rifle.

– That's how I would be too.

– But he can't join the Comanche. He never would anyway. Never. He belittles Mart for being a half-breed. And the end. Oh my god. With Debbie. But the last shot is so iconic. I bet you've seen it, even if you haven't seen the movie. It's everywhere. It's one of the most famous last shots in Hollywood history.

– Don't tell me yet. I want to know how they get there.

– The door frame, and he's walking out on his own, it's really, I mean that image. You've never seen it?

– No and don't tell me. I want you to tell me the whole thing.

– Okay. But the ending, the doorway, it underlines the great tragedy, from the movie's perspective at least. The final sequence is the whole argument of the film – I have a hard time moving away from it. Him, Ethan, being cast out, that this type of man is without a home, belongs nowhere. The film is arguing that, and you can hear it in that Breitbart write-up, he is essential to creating America, creating a nation. You need men like him, like Kit Carson. Angry men, who will fight and stay angry, keep coming so long as the world turns. Otherwise the wild stays wild. They tame enough of it so that civilization can come in behind them. But they themselves, once that's done, they have no options but to retreat back into the wilderness. The movie, it identifies completely with Ethan, with John Wayne, a man who has been abandoned, who is out of time, left behind. Aggrieved.

– But maybe the world does need to go back to the way it was. Maybe it was better. I'm not saying slavery or Nazis or anything like that, but when I think about my father, and his father, and his father. Yeah, maybe. I feel like I can't say anything anymore. It always pisses someone off.

– I mean, that's part of being constantly aggrieved.

– But why rename the airport that was named after him then? Why take down statues? The people who want to take down statues, isn't that rage too? How is that different?

– I think a lot of that anger is justified. And a long time coming.

– All this stuff about privilege and bad men. Look at me. I'm not rich. Like, I'm privileged because I'm a straight white dude.

But I'm not rich, I'm still paying off debts, I don't get handouts, I gotta work.

– Sure, but that's not what I'm talking about. In the book the movie is based on –

– It's based on a book?

– Yes. It's one of the ones I grabbed. Here.

– What's the other one there?

– *Slouching Towards Bethlehem*. Joan Didion.

– Alan LeMay.

– Yes, he wrote the book the screenplay is based on. I picked it up, sort of randomly, at that little used bookstore on the corner. I had read about it on Wikipedia. I think it was two dollars.

– Is it any good?

– Yes, kinda. It's different. Mart is more the focus of the book. And John Wayne's character, he's not named Ethan. It's something.

– It says on the back. Amos.

– Right, Amos. I picked up the book and thought that it would be a trashy, fast read. But it's actually not bad. It's very vivid. And it stays out of its own way. It describes something and lets it be, without annotation or explanation. There are other parts, though. The book spends a lot more time on Mart. But in the movie, maybe it's the actor, the guy who plays Mart, he's not good, exaggerated at all times. Any scene without John Wayne is so cartoonish. In the book, though, Mart's change over the course of the book is subtle and complex in a way the movie isn't interested in. Mart is the hero of the book, not Ethan. Amos, whatever.

– I should read this book.

– You might like it. You want to borrow it? Like I said, it's better than I thought it would be. You can take it when you go.

– I might stay.

– But what I am trying to say: in the book, the two men keep going out hunting, then returning home. Years pass and each time they come back, it's vastly different, and that change is really sad, and human. The end is pretty different too. Amos, John Wayne's character, dies.

– But not in the movie?

– I'll tell you how the movie ends, eventually. But no, he doesn't die. How could John Wayne die? In the book, it's Mart who is left standing. The tragedy of the book is entirely different: Mart had the chance to stay with the woman, he didn't have to go out and hunt for Debbie. But he does, each time, and in the end he's exactly like Amos. He's angry and wild. But the hope at the end of the book is that he can return to civilization, but Amos, Ethan, can't. He has to die. His kind was a dying species anyway, the end of the life cycle. The movie is pretty different. In the movie, at best, Mart is a check against Ethan. We, the audience, we understand something is wrong with Ethan. Or not completely right. The movie doesn't make him a hero, I guess, but it does make him heroic.

– What's the difference?

– I'm just talking out loud. It's not something I can explain exactly.

– Okay.

– It's also the world right now. I think that's what my brain is working through.

– But the movie was made a while ago? When was the movie made?

– 1955 I think. '56?

– Sixty years ago.

– Yes, but that's sixty years of it in the atmosphere, being breathed in.

– Okay, but it's just a movie. I think this has more to do with your dad.

– It's a part of it.

– It's just a movie. I get it. It's important to you. But it is just a movie.

– But movies, art, bring things already present to the surface. But they don't just reflect things. They express things. They wish for things, they desire, they shape desires.

– Okay.

– For example, in the next scene, Mart and Ethan, it's winter and they come across a herd of bison. I think they must be in Colorado or something, and they come across them all feeding. There are so many of them. Watching it, I think about they used to be everywhere. How they travelled in herds of thousands until they were all slaughtered, predominantly by settlers.

– I've seen them in the wild. I have family in Alberta and Saskatchewan. My aunt. And we used to drive from BC a lot, at least a couple of times a year. You have to go through the Rockies.

– And there were bison there?

– I only saw them once, but yes, it was a whole herd. I had seen pictures, but in real life they were all muscle, way bigger. But I was also a kid. But bison, yeah, they still exist.

– How long ago was this?

– Maybe twenty, twenty-five years ago. Yeah.

– A while ago.

– Yeah. But they still exist. They're still there.

– I'm getting at that, though. I'm not saying they are extinct, but they are so far from what they once were. In the movie, they need meat for food. So Mart shoots one. And it's heartbreaking. I think they actually shot a bison in the movie – I don't know how you would fake it, it looks so real. And you watch it crumple to the ground. It doesn't fall over, just sinks straight down, its legs right underneath it. It's heartbreaking.

– They had to eat.

– Sure, okay. After he shoots the one, the herd starts to stampede. It's impressive, seeing all those giant animals in motion. They are really strange creatures when you look at them, especially compared to horses. There're horses all through the movie obviously. Horses. That's part of the joy of Westerns, I think, getting to see horses at their full speed. And they are so elegant, not like the bison, who are so powerful. The bison are stampeding and then John Wayne just starts firing into the herd. He's just firing and firing maniacally. Mart tries to grab his arm and Ethan throws him off, his gun jams and he just picks up Mart's and keeps shooting. And yelling. He's yelling that the Comanche won't have any to eat that winter. He's killing these animals out of spite, out of pure malice. It's not logical. He wants to kill everything. Today, the bison are basically extinct, or wild bison are almost extinct. I read a phrase for it: 'ecologically extinct.' Functionally, in the wild, they are extinct.

– I saw some.

– I know.

– So he shot a bunch of bison. In a movie.

– Right. But it's more than that. I've also been reading this book about Columbine. It was there in the used bookstore and I realized I knew so little about it. The Michael Moore movie, a few newspaper articles, Wikipedia. All I knew was that these two boys started the school-shooting thing.

– I remember them calling us into an assembly the next day. This would have been high school. Grade 11, I guess. The principal gave this big long speech about how sad she was that it happened, that we didn't need to be afraid, and that if we needed someone to talk to about it, there were counsellors. And to keep an eye out for warning signs from other people. It was all over the news too, every day.

– This book is really detailed. It's just called *Columbine*. The author was a reporter at the time. Anyway, the book has some of the killers' journals. Eric, he was the guy who did most of the planning: he had little spreadsheets and methodical to-do lists. He wrote the word EXTINCTION in big letters across one entry. He used the word a lot, in the middle of these long rants about how weak humans are, how so few of us deserve to live. He kept writing NATURAL SELECTION in big letters too. There was a misconception that they targeted jocks or whoever. But no, he wanted to kill everything and everyone. They had this whole plan to set off these huge bombs in the cafeteria. The bombs were there, planted, but they didn't go off. They just wanted as much carnage as possible. Eric had this fantasy he repeated about the total extinction of every human on Earth.

– He sounds crazy.

– The book argues he was a sociopath. Obviously not diagnosed, but still. And he left these long, detailed fantasies of murdering everyone. Literally every person, the whole globe on fire. It wasn't just jocks or nerds or Black kids or Christians or whatever. He wanted everyone dead.

– Crazy. He was crazy. That's not normal. Like that guy who shot all the people on the Danforth.

– I don't think this kind of stuff is only done by crazy people. And now, shooters, they cite the Columbine kids. The van killer, the one who drove through that crowd at Yonge and Finch, he talked about Elliot Rodger, who left that long manifesto about being an incel.

– So John Wayne was crazy?

– That's not what I'm saying. But there is something completely vicious about shooting a herd of bison in order to starve a whole group of people. If he had his way, he would make the bison extinct so that it would bring about the extinction of the Comanche.

– You're reading into it a bit much.

– You were talking. Your friend. The Gakhal family. Didn't that pig farmer murder all those Indigenous women not far from where you grew up?

– Pickton? I mean he wasn't that close. It's like a five-hour drive. I looked at it once, though, yeah, I did drive by that farm going to Vancouver. I would have had to. But no, he wasn't close.

– But all that was around you. It was there when your dad was growing up, and his dad too.

– I just remember there was a local blackout about the trial, for whatever reason. But I would just watch the Seattle news and get all the details.

– I'm not saying there are straight lines between these things. I think Columbine resonates. 9/11 obviously. I'm not saying they are equal, or even that similar. Connected points maybe. But there is something that connects them.

– Come on, the movie has nothing to do with 9/11.

– I just – I don't think I'm explaining it quite right. The way I understand it, the movie expresses ideas that still resonate, that are still important to a large number of people. One of which is a fury, a real pervading, ubiquitous anger. It still matters.

– I just don't see how it relates to 9/11. I remember how strange, fucked up, that morning was. I woke up between the two planes hitting. At first they were talking about how a plane had flown into one of the towers, and it was news, they broke into whatever song, but there wasn't panic. But then the second one, all hell broke loose. And the news kept replaying the one plane flying in, with the tower smoking behind it. That dark smoke, just pouring out, then *bam*. The second plane.

– I'm not trying to say the movie is the same thing as 9/11.

– Then why bring it up?

– It's all a tangle. I'm not sure there is a way to completely explain the whole thing, or to follow every path, every vein. Pickton. It's hard not to think about that when talking about Westerns, especially this one. I'm not an expert, but it's clear that the residential schools, everything, was an effort at extinction. To completely annihilate Indigenous languages and cultures, to destroy.

– Maybe I'm too drunk to follow you.

– It's getting late.

– I can't stay over?

– No, I don't think so.

– But maybe? Yes. I have to know how this movie ends. You have to tell me.

– Can you put the kettle on, please?

– Oh yeah. Here. Okay. Okay. I'll go do it. Whoa.

– Be careful. Everything okay?

– What? Yeah, no, everything is fine. A beer got away from me. It's fine.

– Okay.

– But we were never like that couple? The one fighting on the street?

– Did you put the kettle on?

– Fuck. No. Sorry. I just walked in there and forgot.

– It's okay. I'll do it.

– Sorry. I'm a bit out of it.

– It's fine. It's getting late.

– So how does it end?

– They find Debbie. They rescue her.

– Just like that?

– No.

– Tell me.

– First the American army shows up, just as Ethan is shooting all the bison. It turns out they've just come from their own war-party raid. Ethan and Mart, they double back to see it. When they get there, the village is decimated, bodies and clothes and objects strewn all over. The army destroyed everything.

– It was war. Both sides were doing it.

– Yes, both sides. John Wayne walks through it and you can see the breath of the horses. That is what stands out: the horses' breath and how white everything seems around all the bodies.

– But that is war. That was how it was.

– Ethan figures they probably have prisoners. Maybe Debbie is there or maybe they know where she might be, someone might know. They pass these long lines of prisoners, shivering in the cold, blankets around them, women holding children. The first room, they see two younger girls. They're strangers, not related to Debbie. One of them has a long scar across her forehead, and she can't stop smiling. She doesn't say anything, just has this giant empty grin. John Wayne says something like 'They ain't white anymore.' They are wild too, creatures, non-humans, things. Comanche. The movie is really reductive, straightforward, in some ways. It is an easy movie to understand in many ways.

– It's how the world is.

– I know people think that. I can see it all over the internet.

– Like on Twitter?

– Sure. But I am talking more about 4chan, or 5chan, or Reddit. The wilder parts. That Rodger kid, he uploaded videos to YouTube, but he was also on the beta-male parts of Reddit. And the van killer, he read that Rodger kid there too, online. It's there, in the open, post after post, man after man, who think and feel like him. And it's mostly young men, self-styled victims. Aggrieved and angry. Incels. The amount of hatred for women, it really upsets me. It seems like there are so many of them.

– I'm not like that.

– And they have their own language, their own terminology and shorthands. A whole culture, a whole species of young men.

– Not all of them. A lot of it is just teenagers blowing off steam. Just a bunch of boys.

– But that online world is very straightforward too. The messages are very clear and very visible.

– I think we just disagree. I'm allowed to disagree with you.

– I'm not trying to convince you of anything. I'm thinking out loud. These are things I think about a lot.

– I'm allowed to disagree. Calm down. I don't get blaming John Wayne for 9/11 and Reddit.

– Okay. Let me finish. That's part of the whole movie again, a part of the tragedy the film argues for. Ethan is cast out, he's a victim, he doesn't belong. But he's also the smartest person in the movie. He knows everything, knows every language, every custom, every person, everything. He is a master of everything. He is a survivor. A hero.

– He is a hero.

– But he's also a victim. Martha. His love. His justifications, his cruel streak and his violence, his anger.

– I don't agree.

– Let me finish. So they keep looking. They go down to Mexico because they hear a rumour that Scar is down there. And they meet a man who knows where Scar is. They have a

Mexican guide take them directly into the camp and right away they meet up with Scar. And Scar knows who they are. He shows them Ethan's medal, the one he took from Debbie. Oh god, his voice. John Wayne's, I mean. It is this low rumble, menacing and seductive. His voice. You can hear it when he talks to Scar. Part of it is his drawl, the long way he pulls out vowels. It's purposeful, commanding. Nobody else had that voice. It's a parody now, I guess. Everyone does some version of him now. It doesn't matter. No. I don't. Listen, that's what I'm trying to explain. 'You speak good American.' That's what he says to Scar when they start talking. In that voice. They follow Scar into the tent. Usually only men are allowed into the tent, but he explains that his two sons have been killed, so he has his wives sitting there with him. And then he shows them his scalps. He says that because his two sons were taken from him, he now takes as many scalps as he can. And he shows them this string of them, hung from a stick, right in front of their faces.

– They actually did that, though. With scalps.

– Ethan and Scar. They are both these wandering warriors consumed entirely by vengeance. They have no other purpose, no other home. They are similar at least. It's a slight moment of sympathy, for me anyway. But then one of the wives turns around and it's Debbie. She has her hair in two long dark braids on either side of her head. And those braids are interwoven with bright yarn. She looks stunning. She has a choker around her neck and is wearing a Comanche dress. Maroon and soft, velvety.

– And then they shoot everyone.

– No. They leave. They walk right out. They tell Scar they will be camping on the other side of the creek and he should come to them if he wants to trade. And Scar doesn't murder them either. He easily could have killed them both. He shows them the medal. But there is a respect between them. Recognition maybe. Again, I think it's because they are alike. They know each other intimately. They've been chasing him for five years. And when Mart and Ethan get back to their camp, John Wayne explains that he is going to try to kill them.

– Now we're getting to the good part.

– Suddenly the music swells. Ethan and Mart don't notice but there is someone running over the small sandhill. The music is so happy, it's a bit corny. Debbie runs toward them, and Mart runs across the creek to her. And she starts yelling at them in Comanche, motioning that they need to go. She's furious. 'Don't you remember me?' Mart keeps asking her. Then she does answer in English. 'First I prayed to you: come and get me. But you didn't come. Go! Go! Please.' She tells him that these are her people. It's all based loosely on a true story. The woman Debbie was based on ended up having children with the chief who took her. She ended up loving him and her children very much.

– What is that syndrome? You know, where you fall in love with the guy who kidnapped you?

– Stockholm.

– Yeah. She had Stockholm Syndrome.

– No, I don't think so. It's messy. They didn't find her, and so she had to make a life for herself and survive. A new life. And then maybe she grew to like that new life. What else could she have done?

– Run away. Stab him in his sleep. Shoot him.

– I guess so. But in the movie, in real life, she tells them to go. John Wayne, he yells at Mart to step aside. He aims his rifle right at her, and Mart steps in front, shielding her. Ethan wants to kill her. But then Scar's war party arrives and interrupts them, and she runs off, and Ethan and Mart have to run away. They're outnumbered. They get chased and they ride really hard, one hand on the reins and the other holding on to their hats. They are flattened right against the horses and they are a blur. There is one part, they must have buried the camera in the ground, when the war party, dozens of horses, rides right overtop of it, as if they're coming right off the screen.

– They run away?

– There are too many to fight. And they're fast. Ethan and Mart make it to a cave with a big mound of rocks in front. And then they have a shootout. I'm not sure when, but John Wayne gets shot. He's hurt and Mart looks terrified.

– How do they save Debbie?

– Debbie doesn't want to be saved. She's nowhere to be seen. But the two of them, they fight back. The war party charges in waves, and Ethan and Mart shoot, and a few fall off their horses. Then a few more. Ethan and Mart hold them off. Scar gets shot too, and he falls off his horse, in full headdress. The actors, it's almost like they are getting shot for real, the way they fall. Eventually the war party retreats. They don't leave, though. They go just far enough that they can see the cave. So Ethan and Mart are trapped and John Wayne is shot and bleeding.

– And Debbie is just gone.

– She's not with the war party, no. She's disappeared. The front of the cave is covered by the war party, but the back, it opens up. There's an area that's open to the sky, and so Mart and Ethan escape out the back. They've built a fire in the daytime, and the sun is bright and high. And John Wayne is outside tending to his wound and Mart comes up to him. Ethan has his shirt off and his arm is in a sling. He got hit by an arrow and it's poisoned. He's dying. He knows that he's dying, and he hands Mart a piece of paper. He looks so weary, can barely hand it over to him. Mart reads it to him, and the camera stays on John Wayne, and he's crumpled over, tired and bloody. It's his last will. It says he doesn't have any blood relatives, so he's leaving everything – his brother's house, their cattle, everything – he leaves it all to Mart. Mart is family, there's a change in Ethan, and Mart has a chance to be different. But not John Wayne. Just like the start of the movie, he's giving everything away.

– He's dying.

– That's what he thinks. 'What about Debbie?' Mart says, and throws it back at him. And Ethan answers, with a growl, 'She's been living with a buck.' She's no longer white. And the thing is, he's really good in the scene. There is command in his acting. He is this solid object that the whole scene revolves around. His gravity. Being John Wayne.

– Just manly.

– It's something, I don't know, again, it's something I think about. People who like the movie, who like John Wayne, say it's his best acting. And it is, and it is a performance. A racist one, full of cruelty and anger. And the movie wears that openly and makes no attempt to hide it. There are times where, like when he shoots the bison, Mart frames it as him going crazy, as evidence for his anger, his rage. We are supposed to be on Mart's side, but it's impossible because how can we be against John Wayne? But, I mean what about his racism? Does it argue in some way that the racism, that this furious man at the centre of the movie, is right? I don't know. He still gets to be John Wayne.

– He's an anti-hero.

– Okay. Sure. I do think it makes him a more interesting character. But in some ways, it makes the figure that much more forgivable. We understand Ethan more, he's more sympathetic somehow, and so we forgive him. He doesn't get any less angry or cruel, though. He doesn't act any less racist. He doesn't change.

– So, showing any sort of racism in a movie is wrong.

– Oh god. That's a whole different point. I'm not talking about *Schindler's List* or something. I do think, however, that movies can, and often do, impact their audience, the culture. It's undeniable. I think this is different. I do think it makes an argument, a series of justifications for Ethan. And that we can't separate Ethan from John Wayne.

– Okay. I can disagree.

– Yes, of course. But with what?

– That you can't show racism in a movie. Or a racist. That maybe if you like John Wayne you're a racist.

– That's not what I'm saying.

– I'm not even sure he was a racist. That was his generation. The thing I remember, that I always think of first, he beat cancer. That's why my father admired him.

– There are plenty of people who admired him, admire him. I'm not saying otherwise. There's a good Joan Didion article about him and his cancer. From *Slouching Towards Bethlehem*. It's called 'John Wayne: A Love Song.' Here.

– Maybe I'll borrow this too.

– Yes, okay. Her article, it takes place in the mid-sixties, he is filming some movie, I can't remember the exact title. Anyways, it's him and buddies from his previous films, and there's a vibe to it, the last days of this type of movie, this type of actor, this type of person. This is after his cancer scare, and he's hauling around an oxygen tank. I have to find this part. Okay. Oh, the movie was called *The Sons of Katie Elder*. Anyways. Where is it?

– It's okay.

– No, I'll find it. I have so much of it marked up, with stars in the margins. I'll find it.

– I'll get another drink while you look.

– Another one?

– Just one more. I have to know how it ends. You find it. I'll be right back.

– Okay. I have an early morning tomorrow.

– Did you find it?

– Yes.

– I also brought you a little one to drink. You're welcome. I'm ready. Read it to me.

– 'I had never thought of John Wayne having dinner with his family and with me and my husband in an expensive restaurant in Chapultepec Park, but time brings odd mutations, and there we were, one night that last week in Mexico. For a while it was only a nice evening, an evening anywhere. We had a lot of drinks and I lost the sense that the face across the table was in certain ways more familiar than my husband's.'

– That's good.

– 'As it happened I did not grow up to be the kind of woman who is the heroine in a Western, and although the men I have known have had many virtues and have taken me to live in many places I have come to love, they have never been John Wayne, and they have never taken me to that bend in the river where the cottonwoods grow.'

– Wow.

– She's an incredible writer. The essay starts with her in the 1940s seeing her first John Wayne film, and it's that ghost, that shadow. It makes her sad to see him with the oxygen tank, and it scares her that he got cancer. There is a reality behind him that itself doesn't seem real. But there it is. She has to look. And then she has to reconcile it with her own memories and past.

– I would love to have dinner with John Wayne. Imagine.

– There is some nostalgia. Her essay, it's a love song to someone like John Wayne, his allure. There is an intimacy. She says that his face is maybe more familiar than her husband's. There is love.

– You're not drinking?

– I have a long day tomorrow. We're almost done anyways. I'm tired.

– I can drink yours too then.

– They abandon Debbie. She's left to her own devices, and Ethan and Mart return home. Ethan is still hurt from the arrow.

– So they don't rescue her.

– They get back just in time to see that the girl who had been waiting for Mart is getting married to another man. It's sort of like the book, a turning point, where Mart has turned into Ethan and lost his chance to fit in with the new world. But Mart, he ends up getting in a fight with her new husband. It's kind of dumb. I don't really care about Mart and the romance story. It's dumb and I don't care about it.

– Wouldn't you like it? Two guys fighting over you?

– I just don't care about either of them.

– If anyone ever hurt you, I would totally fight him.

– It's the least interesting part of the movie. The Rangers that are at the wedding, they want to arrest Ethan and Mart, but they find out that Scar is nearby and they want all the men they can get to fight him. They head out again, one last time. John and Mart, because they are criminals, or the Rangers think they are, they don't get guns, and have to be scouts. They go on ahead. The colours of the end sequence, just before the attack, they're incredible. It's all blue-hued. John Wayne stands on this outcropping. He's majestic, and down below him is the badlands, and a bit beyond that is Scar's camp. It's the last time we get to see the desert. It's twilight, the end of the day, and we get to see everything from his viewpoint.

– I really want to go there. We could go.

– Ethan wants to charge in, and he knows they would probably kill Debbie if they did. He doesn't care, he says something like 'Living with Comanche isn't being alive.' But Mart convinces them to at least let him try to sneak in. Mart gets all the way into the camp, all the way to Debbie in Scar's tent. She screams and he covers her mouth. She's changed her mind. When she talks to him, she talks to him in English. She's ready to be saved. Scar bursts into the tent and Mart shoots him dead and they escape. But the gunshots. Ethan and the Rangers think he's in trouble and come riding in hard into the camp. And they murder everyone. They ride through the first time, shooting. They ride all the way through the camp, and the music is triumphant. And then they turn around and do it again, killing anything that's left. There is nothing left. They obliterate it. John Wayne rides up. He has no gun, but he does have his horse, and he rides literally into Scar's tent. He sees Scar's dead body and he still has his knife. It's one of the large hunting knives and he takes it out and he's smiling. He lowers himself, and the camera cuts away, but you know he scalped him.

– His revenge, finally.

– Well, it happens off-screen, but it's horrific. Ghoulish. Scar is dead and that's not enough. Ethan needs more. Then, in all the chaos, Debbie runs off. Ethan rides behind her and she dodges and runs and ends up trapped against a giant rock. He's going to kill her. He's stalking her. He's massive, hulking toward her. She has nowhere to run. He lumbers up to her, no rush at all, slow as he wants. She's so small. But when he gets to her, he sweeps her up, he cradles her in his arms. I don't entirely understand why but he forgives her. He gets to forgive her. For what? And why?

– She changed her mind too. She wanted to be rescued.

– Maybe because he got his revenge on Scar, I don't know.

– He didn't actually kill Scar though.

– No, but he humiliated Scar. He cut him up so that, like before, he has to wander his whole afterlife, restless. His revenge, it's spiritual. It's a completely brutal, cruel act. And maybe that purges him. Frees him. At least enough to forgive Debbie. She's decided to be white again. But I still don't understand his conversion. Does scalping Scar remove, or balance out maybe, the shame of Debbie? She's made clean again, forgivable. The world is balanced maybe?

– He's the hero. He rescued her.

– I don't know. He definitely comes home the hero. The ending is shot so lovingly. There is real adoration and warmth. I'm not just talking about the music, but the celebration of Debbie coming home. They ride up in a group, but John Wayne and Debbie are at the very front. She is curled into the front of him on his horse, nestled in, protected. Then there's the most famous sequence, the ending.

– Not *True Grit*?

– The end of this movie gets discussed way more. He rides up and people are waiting on the porch for them. Debbie is still in his arms as he gets down, he carries her, then sets her so gently on the ground. There is so much care in that gesture. This mountain of a man tamed enough, just enough, to rescue Debbie, forgive her, and return her. You see both sides of him.

Or at least enough of the soft, light side to make the dark, brutal side tolerable.

– And that's the famous part?

– No. Debbie goes inside. Then Mart and everyone else follows. The camera is in the shadows of the house, looking out through the front door. It's a lot like the opening, with Martha in the doorway. They all walk back into the house so that it's just John Wayne in the desert by himself. But he doesn't follow them inside. He turns and takes a few steps. His walk, that walk. There is dexterity and balance and grace. His head is hung a bit, he's looking down. His back is to the camera, he's walking away into the desert. There is nothing else. No horses. Nothing but the horizon and the dust and him, alone. He walks out alone and the door closes and the film ends.

– The end? That's it?

– He's still the outcast, the victim. Only now he has our total sympathy. He doesn't fit, he doesn't belong. His code, his way of living and being, it's too much for the civilized world. He has that brutal, cruel streak that runs all the way through him. But the world still needs men like him: I think that is what the movie is arguing. They're essential to the world's workings. Whatever he has done is justified, but it costs him exile.

– I think it's sad.

– I don't know. Maybe that's what I meant when I said you reminded me of John Wayne. He's a figure, a set of feelings, that a lot of people identify with. A lot of people think there is something heroic in that brutal streak. The irony then is that he's not an outcast. There are scores of people, men, who all believe this. They do have a home. He's not an island. He's a nation.

– That's it?

– That's the end.

– You think I'm like that. Brutal?

– Please don't. You've been drinking.

– You didn't always think that. We used to do this a lot more. We used to stay up all night and talk. What about those times?

– We were younger then. I had more energy, more space. Maybe more tolerance. Or I didn't know better.

– But you've changed.

– I think everyone's changed. It's just a fact of getting older.

– Changed for the better?

– I like myself more now, yes. Does that make sense?

– But I do miss the old you. The one I first met.

– It was a long while ago.

– We were good together. At least admit that.

– We had some good times. We were younger then too.

– And now you've outgrown me?

– No. I didn't mean that. Just I had more energy for certain things when I was younger.

– And now?

– Now, no.

– No?

– It's getting late.

– I get it, yeah, you're tired.

– I'm exhausted.

– Here, let me help. I'll help.

– No, it's fine. I'll clean up in the morning. It's late.

– Sure.

– I'll go get your coat.

– Oh. I thought I was staying over.

– I have a long day tomorrow. I have to get some sleep and be out of here early.

– You don't want me to stay.

– Not tonight, please.

– I'll sleep on the couch.

– Another night.

– Sure. Whatever.

– Please don't be angry.

– I don't get it.

– I'm sorry, the gun.

– I came all the way here. You invited me.

– I've just got to get to sleep. I need to sleep.

– Well, it's not like we're going to fuck. You've made that clear.

– Please.

– I would just sleep on the couch here.

– I'll go get your coat. Please.

– Okay. Fine. Fine. Fuck. I've got a long walk home. Thanks.

– I'm sorry. Here.

– I won't be home until, when?

– I'm sorry.

– I sat and listened to you all night. Isn't that worth something?

– I'm sorry.

– All right I'm going. All right. How does this lock work? All right. Fine.

– Goodnight.

– Whatever.

SONS

'John Wayne looked down and stared stupidly at the arrow in his thigh, shaking his head in amazement and disbelief as two bullets ripped through his chest and out the back of his jacket.'
— Thomas King, *Green Grass, Running Water*

'It was a thick pervasive fog – tumbling and yellow. Amber. It was diseased. It exuded poisonous odours and fetid, unidentifiable smells of the kind that came from the earth, as if it had been digging there in cemeteries and thick lagoons of human waste... Because of this, there was a roaring trade in surgical masks for those who could make their way to stores and hospitals. But, in time, the supplies ran out and the people reverted to the old-west style – a city of frontier bandits done up in red and blue bandanas.'

— Timothy Findley, *Headhunter*

MONDAY

*H*e didn't realize that the windows had been shaking until he inserted his key into the door of his apartment, locking it. He can't remember exactly how he got to his door, the small weight of the key flexing in his hand, but he pivots down the hallway, past the familiar dark marks scraping the light walls, past the doors of his neighbours, equidistant from one another, repetitive and modular. He does remember late last night: he drank beer until he started yawning and nodding in front of his TV, was jolted awake by yelling out on the street, a fight rising up to the window of his apartment, her voice at him, and he thought of Melanie from two nights ago, her bright lips, the snick of her lock after she closed the door on him. He got up then, fought his way through the bottles piled around the couch, to his bathroom; he remembers inspecting his features, a bit sunburned, hard, drunk eyes, while he was brushing his teeth, and the lingering mint in his mouth. There had been a text, a few hours earlier, that still made him angry, telling him they didn't need him for his Monday shift, and that brought him down to only twenty-five hours that week. Then a chasm of missing time before he remembers being awake at his door the next morning, rotating his key in the knob. Now he is walking down the hall to the elevator and bits of sensation emerge from his fugue: his bedroom windows were vibrating loud enough to wake him up, a tuning-fork frequency, drawling and low, that first resonated in his chest, then dipped to his stomach. Then, in his memory, he is at his door again, awake and in his hall.

A door opens behind him, then another, and when he turns the corner to the elevator there are already three people waiting. A couple about his age lean against one another: he has a healing cut above his right eye and his hair is uncombed, and he hasn't put his right foot fully into the shoe, his heel is slipping out; she wears a plain large T-shirt that expands and swallows her and nearly all of her shorts, just the hem of denim visible, her over-thin wrists disappearing behind the man as her arm wraps around his waist. He sees that the man has a scar running from his eye to his lip that quivers when he talks; they whisper something he can't hear before the man nods and they both eye the elevator in anticipation. The third person is facing away, her hair grease-wet, and she turns back to the elevator, then away from it, looking down the opposite hall, pacing. He pauses and looks at the trio, then makes brief eye contact with the woman pacing, her eyes spooked in semi-panic and her mouth stretched into a giant empty grin. She stops and her eyes recede slightly as if she is withdrawing into her own mind. Through her eyes, he realizes, he must look large and intimidating, his wide body, the spread of his large hands.

He decides then against the elevator, navigates around the couple, toward the staircase, the suction of the door's light resistance. Then he's descending, gripping the metal handrail before the stairs flatten to the third-floor entrance. As he makes his way down, he can hear footsteps above him, other people voicelessly flowing downward through the concrete echo of the stairwell, the rumbling vibration of the windows still wormed into his body, making him unsteady. The hangover that had been crouching quietly in his body unfurls itself and he has to watch his feet carefully, and the footsteps, doubling, tripling above him as more residents descend, he feels them chasing him and hustles past the second-floor door. He reaches the first floor as the chorus of people coming down grows; he can hear voices now among the echoes as he enters the open lobby. Eyeing the glass and sunlight of the front doors, he crosses past the security guard's empty station. The elevator behind him sounds and begins to open as he pushes outside, toward the sirens, two fire trucks, then an ambulance, that are blurring past, toward the city centre.

To the left, along Dundas East, there is a streetcar stopped just past the Sherbourne intersection; the driver has opened the doors between stops and people are spilling out onto the sidewalks. He looks to his right, following the undulating walls of emergency vehicles' wailings; there is the top of a column of darkening smoke rising above the skyline, a sheer formation, solid, and yet, as he keeps watching, he sees how it drifts apart at its edges as it disperses into the hot summer morning, the colours of a desert sunset against a mountain horizon, almost beautiful if it were not so terrifying. The cloud spreads, a palm unbunching from fist to flat, but a total view is semi-obscured by the low buildings and the western curve of Dundas. There is a group of men at the corner of Pembroke, men who he sees only late at night when they stumble out of the bar as he comes back to his apartment. They are usually glassed with beer, arguing in clumps and smoking each other's cigarettes as they sit in the doorways of the neighbouring businesses stringed along the north side of the street: a bodega, a dry cleaner, a beauty salon, each with barred gates and iron shafts over their windows. The few times he has gone in for a beer, the men immediately turned to him, predator eyes glinting, marking him as foreign; they moved deliberately away until he hunched over the bar and finished whatever bottle was the cheapest.

These same men were now out in late-morning light, and in that brightness he moves toward them. One man, sweaty with dirt-smudged socks, dark-skinned from sun, stands next to him holding a bottle that he swings by the neck to his lips. The slope of the street gives him a clearer view, and the crowd around him all look together along the same sightline: past the tall, new condo complex, advertising central air conditioning and a free parking spot, past the construction cranes crossed and mid-use; they look past the half-glass skeleton of another new building, the bright windows along its bottom against the concrete bones of the top. If not for the buildings to give it scale, the smoke might be rising from the ruins of a horse stable or some small cabin; the intensity of the billowing cloud suggests the burning of hay and dry wood, raging upward in a tight, pitch-coloured monument, and now he can also see lighter, sporadic puffs around its column that are parallel to the main pillar and cement grey. He wonders if the dark smoke isn't a fire and the silvery bursts aren't something collapsing. The late summer months of his childhood were filled with forest fires, which looked like this one, he thinks, and the smoke rising from downtown is like the burning that would smother the valley, turning the sun fluor-escent and apocalyptic.

He stands and watches the scene, and it barely moves: it is a film still, then a movie in extreme slow motion where minute parts are morphing. One block down, he sees the tableau outside Filmore's strip club, its facade with the towering neon letters, the 'O' and 'R' refusing to light. Past that, there is the hotel out the back of the club that he has heard snickers about, the dancers or other women who will bring clients back there, grabbing their hands and pulling them out of the lights and poles and music of the space. He is pulled from this fantasy back into his body by a young woman, blond hair tied in a long braid down her back, bright yarn interwoven, talking to what looks like a bouncer; both of their backs are to him because everyone is facing the same direction, to the city's core, toward the surreal near-stasis, a warping limbo moving in slow motion. When he pulls his eyes upward to the smoking cloud, continuous and strong and dark, he realizes how hot it is, the breeze lightly blowing but humid and gritty, as if a fine dusting of sand is settling on his skin. He reaches his fingers up and they come back silty and slick, and then he is suddenly aware of the small streaks of wet dampening the mid-back of his red-and-blue-checkered shirt. His headache expands, blooms in this heat; the sky is a fake overblue, Technicolor, and the sun burns in the middle of it. The whole summer has been like this: days, weeks of people waiting for evening cool, the ever-present smell of proximity, to others, to rotting food, to garbage, the smells amplified by the heat. The air still retains the humid weight of the day before's early-evening rain, when he had been out getting tall cans of cheap German beer, the bag against his thigh as he ran through the storm, rushing inside and upstairs – his shirt was soaked through and he threw it into the corner of his bathroom, stripped off his socks, pants. The rest of the night was spent drinking and moving around his apartment in his underwear, watching the movie, her movie, both hot and chilled, the foam of the beer fading after the first few sips, then another beer, another. On the street, he remembers, there was a couple fighting in the rain, a woman pleading for the man to leave, and he thought of Mel then, now, and wanted to apologize. Then, just as suddenly, he flashes to a moment during his furious walk home from her apartment two nights ago, east along College, when he seemed to pass under the shade of a large tree, a respite from the swelter, where the heat and the fever of his anger broke, and he exhaled with relief. He paused then, his head swimming with bourbon and residual fury: an orange-and-green cab drove by with its light on, and then someone laughed on a street somewhere just south and out of view, a woman, and everything rushed back,

Mel describing the movie, her handing him his coat, his leaving. He stamped forward home again and woke up the next morning determined never to text her again, but to watch the movie, John Wayne, that night and get very drunk. The desert of the movie hangs in his mind, its vistas and harsh architecture of monumental stones that backdrop Ethan and his horse as he rides, an image that lingers as he brings himself back from the memory, blends with the present, the heat of this morning, the crowd around him, and the glistening and growing cloud rising from the city's centre.

He is startled by the realization that more people have gathered uncomfortably around him, mixed in with the men from the bar, and the stalled traffic. He instinctually puts his hands into his pockets and turns, past a woman holding two plastic grocery bags: he can see the bright colours of a cereal box in one, the off-brand carton of juice in the other. Beyond her shoulder, through the bar's window, he can see an angled TV: there is a text scroll along the bottom, red with white lettering, but the glare of glass distorts it so he can only see the word LIVE in the right corner; underneath, a wide shot of a large smouldering hole, grave-like, with rich smoke, from the middle of wreckage, and jets of water spraying into its centre, steady red-blue flashes farther beyond the perimeter. The camera swings around, but the movement and the glare and the angle of the screen make it impossible to gauge the scale of the event: the fire trucks now look tiny, and the fire shifts to an unreal massive size, the buildings and people and fire and vehicles pooling, and then there is a uniformed woman in the corner who looks to be twice the size of the police car she's standing next to. Then the footage cuts to what looks like a replay: there are flames to the left of the building, and he focuses his eyes, tries to place it, a bank building perhaps;

then the fire encroaches, the camera rocks suddenly with an explosion, and the building leans. He thinks he sees a large object jutting perpendicular to the building, as if it crashed there, before the structure's top floors begin to collapse onto the streets below, and suddenly there are people running toward the camera in panic, being chased by a cloud of dust and smoke. The camera jolts, then transitions to more footage, gathered by a cellphone: there is debris falling from off-screen and down, and then, on-screen, more flames. This image lingers as the orange and yellow swallow the trees planted in front of the building, become blazing pyramids, before a blur interrupts; to him it looks like a dress, unbodied and charred, that has been flung across the camera's view, blurred in freeze frame.

His temples thunder and he is suddenly starving, the bite of his stomach gnaws and last night's drinking lashes at his eyes so that the TV screen melts incomprehensibly. *I need food, time to figure out what is happening,* and her name comes to him again. *She must be terrified.* Turning away from the downtown, the smoke, he goes east against the horde of people, looking from face to face as he moves: there is a young Chinese man he recognizes from his building, shy with his insecure English, and he seems very young in the sunlight, more of a boy; there is a woman he recalls from Sam's, the small convenience store across the street, moving through the same aisles as him, mirroring his choices in sparse groceries, instant soup, two apples, a loaf of bread; there is a father holding a small girl, a green Band-Aid on her knee, a locket dangling from a thin chain bobbling against her shirt; the girl grabs the chest of the man, bunching his shirt. He and the father make brief eye contact as he goes past, and the father tenses into a defensive position, grim, and there is sweat around the frames of his glasses as he hops the girl in his arm, then shifts her to the other side of his body, his other hand a fist. The girl's head follows him as he moves on, past his apartment building entrance, the beauty college, Avola, past the initial striking purple of the True Love Café and into its open side door. There is a man behind the counter near the back of the building and he's pointing at a muted TV screen just out of eyesight behind the wall that separates them from the kitchen.

'Oh, sorry.' The owner grabs one last look at the screen and comes toward him. 'Pretty crazy, huh? I felt the building shake. They're saying it might've been an earthquake.'

'An earthquake?'

'Yeah. A big one. I was here a few years ago when they had that one up in the Ottawa Valley. 5.2. Was just sitting here and all the mugs started shaking. Weirdest sound.' The owner puts one hand on his bald head. 'It's so hot.'

'Yeah. That rain last night didn't help at all.'

'No.' He motions his head toward the oversized fan stationed near the front door. 'That's the best we can do.'

'Better than nothing.' He looks at the chalk-written menu on the far wall and orders the Juicy Sexy Burger, no tomato, and a Coke Zero. He catches the owner lingering as he grabs the drink from the fridge, stealing a bit of cool air before handing the can to him.

'I'll bring it out to you.'

'No rush.' He walks toward a table near the fan, next to a flowing leafy plant and against the window looking out onto Dundas. There is a man in the corner of the restaurant at one of the three old computers: he bites at a sandwich from a nearby plate, then goes back to pecking at the keyboard. He can glimpse part of the man's screen and is startled to see the writhing of naked bodies, one of which looks blood-smeared, a man holding a long weapon, like a lance, over someone prone; he begins to stand, to confront him, looking back to the owner, but when he looks back, the computer screen is filled with a Facebook feed, and the man is scrolling downward, barely pausing. *Did I imagine or*, and then a vision of the cloud, downtown, comes into his head, and he wonders if there are some sort of chemicals in it, something that might cause him to hallucinate.

He continues watching the man, considers the loud hum of the computer's fan, then sits, pulls out his phone: a text from his mother: *Everything okay? Just watching it on the News.* He closes the text app without answering and opens Twitter, reads the trends: *Toronto, #PrayforToronto, #416, Business District, #TorontoStrong*, then scrolls through the first wall of tweets, from @CP BREAKING: *Toronto Fire trying to bring downtown explosion under control*, from @CBC *Possible Earthquake Hits Downtown Toronto*. This repeats as he pulls his finger down in a petting motion, refreshing wary scraps of information, pictures of fire trucks, photos from personal accounts, one from the other side of orange barricades, cordoned off, that shows the edges of a fire from blocks away, a police officer with one palm out in front of him but head turned in the same direction as the camera; he sees the video again that ends with the charred dress, replays it two more times, trying to decide what that final blurred object is; there is a short, shaky video of someone running, and he stares at it and catches a glimpse of a semi-open plaza, a hazily familiar building made strange by a river of distorting smoke flowing between it and the camera, before a cop on horseback gallops across, then the footage is moving too fast, and the clip runs out. *There is nothing about the air, about seeing things, but.*

The man in the corner leans in his computer chair noisily, making an irritated noise, and lets his hands fall heavily on the keyboard. They see each other for a moment, and the man's pupils are dilated, growing past the whites of his eyes; the man grins, waves. He returns the wave cautiously, and the man returns to his computer.

'Here you go.' The owner puts the plate down, a wooden serving platter with two brass handles on either side.

'Great.'

'They're still saying maybe earthquake?'

'I guess. I don't know.'

'I guess so then. Your change. You forgot it.' He places the coins on the table just as two women come in the front door, pause, and look expectantly. 'I'll be right there,' the owner adds in their direction. The light gleams off the coins' overly shiny silver surfaces; he picks up the nearest quarter, taking in its unmarred faces, bright as if freshly minted.

He pockets them and opens his text app again, tapping to his last conversation with Melanie, two days ago. *Come on up.* He opens up Instagram, to his private messages, to a conversation from a week ago when he had sent her a post about a bar near her and an offer to buy her a drink; she had responded that they should just hang at her place and he should text her. He sees that she was active six minutes ago, but when he moves over to her account there are no new photos; he scrolls down, pausing on the posts with her face in them. There is one he has always liked: she is at a work function, wearing a baby-blue dress that is pulling up her thighs, with a soft cottonwood-coloured scarf falling off her shoulders, like a bending river, her neck in profile, her slightly twisted posture revealing a small bow on the back of the dress. He moves to his Messenger app, sees that she has a green dot next to her profile, taps; they've never spoken on there and he hovers his thumbs above the keyboard, then types,

I'm sorry about the other night. Are you okay? then erases it. He remembers the half of her face, pristine but haughty, before she closed the door on him, then the silent hallway lurching with the remnants of the bourbon firing in his mouth. He was thinking of her as he watched the movie last night, followed the horses sprinting across the desert, the drawl of John Wayne, the pistols firing. The images moved past him and he thought of his father, his feet set underneath him, picking off bottles in the woods, his large shoulders absorbing the recoil. When he first saw Martha, he thought of Melanie's expressive eyes, flickering with tenderness and forgiveness, before he remembered and was overtaken by the memory of the half of her face resting against her door jamb, then the door closed and he was alone.

Placing his phone beside him on the table, he grabs the burger with both hands; he bites and the beef begins to break apart, and he rushes to place it back down, one large blood-like blob of ketchup on the protruding lettuce. He looks out the window and across. Barely visible around the nose of the stopped streetcar, there is a bank of four battered pay phones with giant yellow arrows above them pointing down. The phones are all occupied: there is a man all the way on the left who is propping his bike against himself, an aqua handkerchief leaking from the cargo pocket of his pants; he's shirtless and his tattoos scrawl up his skin, from the back of his shoulder blade around over the top to his chest, the exact design indistinct, a weaving of letters or a series of intertwined dragon-type creatures visible as he waves his hand above his head. There is a woman in business attire next to him, her bag under one arm, and the TTC driver next to her, monitoring his abandoned vehicle, and a man next to him, leaning to his side with a briefcase between his polished dress shoes. The last two are positioned so that they are looking at each other as they talk, as if in conversation, and he wonders why anyone is using the pay phones at all, why the TTC driver isn't using his radio. He pushes the button to wake his phone, brings up his home screen and the carrier information is blank, five empty dots and an E where the 5G should be. People queuing for the pay phone now.

'I don't know. I mean maybe. I don't know.'

'My friend out in Scarborough didn't feel anything. No tremors or anything.'

The women are seated two tables over, within the path of the fan. The brunette facing him checks her phone and twists her mouth. 'Do you have reception?'

'Weird. No.' The other woman puts her phone back in her purse, the bag yawning open on one of the empty chairs beside her. 'Yeah, so, Trina said she didn't feel anything this morning.'

'I think it must be some gas leak. That's what the radio was saying.'

'Oh, like that guy in Mississauga. Blew him and his wife up in their house.'

'Did you actually see pictures of that?'

'Yeah. The house was completely destroyed. Everything was wiped out and they couldn't find any of her body, their bodies. Can you imagine?'

'This thing downtown seems bigger, you know? That smoke, it doesn't seem like it's stopping any time soon.'

He considers the texture of the burger as he listens to them talk.

'Yeah, it was definitely an explosion, I think. Earthquakes don't feel like that.' The brunette lights up her phone again. 'Still nothing.'

He retraces today's waking moments, back to his front door, reverses the key from the lock and tries to relive waking up, putting on his shoes, and leaving his bedroom: there is blankness, nothing except the feeling of the shudder of his windows, the shaking in his guts, but even that sensation is disembodied, reverberations and echoes without any other sensation or image attached. He almost says it out loud, the thought is so strong: he wishes he had been awake for whatever happened. He wants to have not missed it, to have lived through it so that he could tell others what it had been like, how he rushed out to the street to look, braving the stampeding crowds and the unknown; he wishes that he were right on the edge of the flames, within the immediate impact. In his fantasy, he is at the centre of the carnage and wreckage, the violence of it, and is now recounting it calmly, under the glistening, rapt attention of an audience, Melanie's vivid eyes.

'I think I'm just going to go home. I was thinking I might go get my nails done later but no. Not now,' the brunette says.

'I'll walk with you. Can I stay for a bit at your place? Ajay's not off work till seven.'

He uses the fork and knife to finish the disintegrating burger, the bites drifting in distracted motions to his mouth, his chewing slow. There are hordes of people on the sidewalk now, *Herds of cattle*, as he notices that the flow of the crowd seems to have reversed and is moving away from the city centre. No one is running, but the massive crowd flowing east is picking its way around the others turned west like sentinels toward the cloud. There is a woman with a long scarf wrapped around her head and around the front of her face, just her eyes visible, the turquoise-and-red streaks against the purple, the colours bursting around her face, but her shirt and pants are spotted with some grey gunpowder substance, wipe marks down the thighs like the scorch marks left behind by fired bullets; the scarf is parts hijab, veil, filter. The man behind her has the same dust on his clothes, walking east as well.

Standing up, he grabs his empty plate and cutlery, returns them to the order counter, nodding to the server, who is looking back over his shoulder from his fixation on the kitchen TV, then exits out the side door. The sidewalk is thick with bodies heated by stress and summer sun, and he surveys from the doorway for the best path away from the smoke, east with the surging waves of dust-coated people: he ducks around another woman, walking through the traffic passing the streetcar on its right, slowly, spilling back into the intersection; he passes a dark SUV and inside there is a young man with sunglasses staring straight ahead, a radio muffled by the passenger window, but he hears 'Police and fire responding' and then he is on the other side of the street.

He steps past the entrance of the Corner Mart, and there is a drooped man immobile against the first window, nearly blocking the advertisements and rates for cheap long-distance calling cards. Another man bumps against the slumped man's leg, but he doesn't move, remains corpse-still, his eye sockets dark hollows, as if shot out. Behind the man, the third window of the Corner Mart facing the street has been replaced by two horizontal pieces of plywood, sunworn and light. The wood has new graffiti messages almost daily, he's noticed, messages layered one on top of the other, sedimentary: the upside-down manufacturing information, dates in computerized slants, then three heavy black Ts in thick spray paint; over this is a thin pastel-purple *Stop violence against women + trans people*, then, in the exact centre there is a small piece bracing the two together and in the same handwriting, clearly, *Reclaim the Streets*. Suddenly he feels each of his senses heightened: all the fuzz of his daily routines and last night's hangover have burned away, and he can see each of the small grains and knots of the plywood, can hear an ambulance south and east, blocks away. He last felt this way, this sensitive, with his father, when they would go fishing or shooting, where his father would tell him about survivalists who would disappear and live off the forest and rivers, men who would trap and hunt and live far away from strip malls and coffee shops. His father would admire 'those men,' and suddenly he could smell the moss on a tree metres away, could feel the slight change in the wind as it moved toward the coppery smell of lake water.

Another fantasy overtakes him, one where he is being interviewed, staring into the camera and fearlessly describing how he navigated his neighbourhood, knowing the exact hidden paths to bypass the panic of the main streets. He rehearses in his mind: no, he did not stay inside and hide and wait, he had to go out and do something, even if it was terrifying and chaotic, he had to be there, he knew no other way. In his imagination, all the details, the sensations bombarding him, are incredibly important; it is his job to notice, to record, he reasons suddenly, so when people look back on this day, they will have all the information available to them, every detail and texture, and he will be the expert.

He's pulled from this image by the noise of shouting: there is another figure jaywalking between cars, stalking; 'I need what I need,' he yells as he heads to the church across the street, the peak of the roof and its triangle windows, a series of long buildings taking up most of the block, the tan stones and faded charcoal-colouring stark against the surrounding monochromatic apartment buildings. The man angles to the middle church building, darker and the brickwork more obvious. Its roof is a harsh spire, its doors a deeper brown, giant, and above them a green-and-white sign offering drop-ins, the name *Margaret* in cursive. The agitated man shouts, 'We buried her, then you went off looking,' and throws something past a couple sitting near the centre's doors – a rock that bounces off the walls – then turns toward him. Even across the street, he notices the stranger's muscles coiled with tension, his neck hard, and the man picks up a discarded McDonald's cup and hurls it overhand down the sidewalk; he watches the man, and his own body balks with threat, his teeth bearing down into a grimace.

This city, he thinks before a sequence from *Taxi Driver* comes to his mind; he's looking through the cab's windshield and the moving colours, impressionistic, and then he remembers Bickle and his monologue. He likes to watch it on YouTube when he's getting ready for work: 'Someday, a real rain will come and wash all this scum off the streets.' He becomes aware of a large truck idling down near the laundromat; the heavy rumble of it adds to the heat, thickening the air, and he stands rigid, the throaty grumble strangely familiar, like the shudder of the windows that woke him that morning; it's so intimate to him that he wonders if he's always lived with that frequency inside him without noticing it, with that quaking and all his muscles tensed in proper simultaneity.

He looks west and the smoke is wider, and the silvery puffs are no longer sporadic: the grey mushrooms around the pouring black are expanding, as a giant rock had been dropped from a great height into the dust of a desert. He breathes deeply. The traffic is completely stopped now; cars have pulled as far over to the curb as they can, their drivers standing beside them, and the chalky crowd moves like ghosts, eastward and weaving between the stopped cars, the sidewalks overflowing. Another deliberate long inhale and the cloud enters him and circulates. Above the church, a flock of birds swirls, spirals in and around the tips of the building. As he watches, the birds morph from a smudge to a face whose flesh drops off into a skull with a gaping mouth; the skull moves its mouth at him, and he can almost hear its words, his father's voice in his hospital bed, struggling to be heard over the machines keeping him alive, but then the shape is birds again, wings and beaks emerging and distinct against the cobalt sky, and then the flying throng is moving toward the lake, south.

How would I explain that? Again, he thinks of the cloud – some sort of psychoactive, obviously: the man at the computer and the gory pornography, the birds. *I don't care if it, the air, is making me see things.* He looks at the spreading black, ash and chemical. *I want it.* His eyes throb and his stomach burbles, and he revisits the image of the skull, a speaking death mask, before last night leaks in: he had passed out on his couch, a beer half-drunk in his hand, and the beer fell over as he slept and spilled onto his legs, waking him; the TV was an unearthly blank blue, and he pulled himself up, patting at the wet, and then he went into the bathroom, brushed his teeth. He had finished the movie, the silhouette of John Wayne, back turned and leaving.

Now he checks his phone to see there's still no reception, and then there is more shouting near Filmore's, and the rising angry voices push him north, opposite; he's near the doors to the William Dennison Apartments, its facade also erratically missing letters, and has to step aside to let out an elderly woman leaving the building; he hurries past her to the unlabelled lane that runs perpendicular to Dundas and along the east side of the building. As he aims up the alley, he watches a TV van move slowly toward downtown, honking; the person in the passenger seat is waving a bright yellow cloth out the window, *dandelion*, Melanie correcting him, and the van bellows, the driver leaning out the window and yelling at the people to move. *Mel*, he considers with fresh urgency, she is in danger. *She must need help.* He tries his phone again, stuffing it back in his pocket with frustration when he sees he still has no signal, then turns north down the alley, across the city, to her.

The beginning of the alley is lined with tall chain-link fences on the left, old mattresses hidden behind them next to stacked wooden pallets. A few steps along, he crosses two dumpsters: the first is black and closed tight, but the rust-coloured second appears to be on the edge of boiling, the heaped black and white plastic bags steaming. A liquid drips down the far side onto a pile of clothes and rags, fuchsia-, navy-, corn-coloured fabrics, and puddles under an abandoned stroller with a leaning left wheel, a cardboard box with glinting beer cans in its seat.

He hears voices around the corner on the right, a man first. 'Has to be, right? Has to be.'

'Yeah, the sound of it. I was near there when it happened, down getting food there. Then this thing, and then people were running away,' a woman replies, holding a backpack in front of her, rummaging through it to its bottom.

'Why were you all the way there?'

'I left my stuff up near Allan Gardens,' the woman answers, scratches the back of her arm, and they both turn to face him. There is an overturned couch next to the pair, and the white grated shelf of a refrigerator propped against it.

'What the fuck,' the man barks at him.

'Nothing.'

'Then keep moving.'

'Yeah, fucking move,' she adds.

'Okay,' he mutters. *A real rain.* Looking ahead: a long stretch of faded brick interspersed with corroded doors, then the metal mouth of a loading dock; the right side of the alley is strung with leaning garages that back onto houses, but every backyard he looks into is empty, the furniture unpopulated, the windows all curtained closed, with patches of garbage between weeds, lights, ripped glinting of chip bags, dogshit. Then the fencing ends and is replaced by back entrances and balconies to apartments, blocky steps and meshed-in porches that lead to weak-looking doors. There are people on nearly every set of metal stairs, in conversation. A young mother is speaking, three children weaving around her, with two other women: 'There were people trapped in the subway but the TV can't interview any of them, I just,' and then she is fragmented by the ringing of a jackhammer in one of the yards on the right; he thinks it sounds like it's coming from near a large parked truck farther ahead, a giant crane protruding from its bed, blocking nearly the whole alley. The jackhammer thumps unseen, and when it stops he hears another conversation, two men, shiny with sweat, one wiping along his eyebrows with his left hand: 'And my brother works down there near one of the buildings but he can't even,' and then the jackhammer again, louder as he approaches it. After the dozen apartments in this part of the alley, at the very left is what looks like a fusebox that has broken open, its grey doors thrown wide and the tentacles of cables doubling and tripling over each other, then split and resplit, bare and brazenly winding into nearby windows. Under the 'No Dumping' sign on the right is a haphazard mound, three mattresses distorted and topped by spare lumber, the outline of a seatless chair, a broken pair of eyeglasses, an abandoned saddle with leather strips sprayed around it.

Then he's past, to a shared courtyard where all the people are clustered around a table. He can hear a radio: 'unclear whether this is a specific attack or whether there is,' then the jackhammer, then a female voice: 'I knew this was going to happen. I was telling you yesterday that'; the radio: 'and police, at this point, are not responding to requests to talk, citing the scale of the incident and the manpower needed to'; over the din of the radio is a different voice, less shrill but still loud, on the cusp of yelling: 'Yes, and this is what happens when we let people, other people from other countries, come into – '

He listens to this jumble as he looks back over his shoulder to see that the pair from earlier are following him, a hundred metres or so back; initially, neither is paying any attention to him, but then he stares too long and the woman catches him, giving him a small sarcastic wave. He pulls his eyes forward, reorienting: there is a crumpled empty cigarette package at his feet and a Popeye's takeout container streaked with thin, reddish hot sauce. When he reaches the large truck, he slips sideways and around its driver's side and sees four men landscaping the back of a two-storey house, one shovelling dark soil into a flowerbed, another with a wheelbarrow moving toward him; the jackhammer sounds from the side of the house, and he watches another man shattering cement, and then there is the last, stepping into a brown porta-potty, the door closes and the man with the shovel pauses to pull from a large bottle of water, briefly making eye contact. As he drinks, his companions halt their work, turn toward him, their arms dangling at their sides, each twitching their trigger fingers, about to draw, and he blinks hard, *The skull, the lance, the cloud*, as he starts to jog away from them. *What else will I see?*

He can see the end of the alley now and the buildings change, grow more squat and solid; looking behind him, he sees the men have returned to their work, the jackhammer and shovels, and he calms slightly. He pauses to catch his breath, takes in the porches and their windows lined with potted plants and multi-coloured glass suncatchers, soon replaced by walls of darker brick as he moves farther north. There is a blue sign with two blocks of small, unreadable white text and, in yellow, a CCTV symbol, the diagram of camera pointed down on him. Behind that sign the round half-sphere of the camera snatches the whole area with its fisheye. He is on camera, he realizes, he is being watched; he imagines seeing himself, then Melanie seeing him through that camera, towering, broad, commanding, how he looks on-screen, how he needs to act. He stands straighter, taller, and considers returning to the construction workers, suddenly angry at himself for fleeing. But then a vision of Mel huddled over her laptop, alone and scared in her apartment, sparks, and he walks purposefully toward Gerrard Street. There are PVC pipes along the right that lead from the inside of the building, then simply end in midair, MRM in dripping paint on one; a stretch of concrete under the brickwork is covered in capital letters, FUCK CANADA, the CA scribbled over but still visible. Above him three large paned windows hover: he can see only the edges of what look like empty bottles on the sills, but the glass itself is clouded over with the reflection of the wide sky. He thinks he sees the streak of a person, then a smaller shadow joins, a father and his son, the child gesturing for him to leave, *Go! Go! Please!* The larger of the two ghostly outlines looms suddenly, triples and rises massive in response. Then, almost instantaneously, both are gone, out of vision. There is the muffle of glass breaking, as if a picture frame falling from the wall, and he waits, but there is no more movement and only silence.

He keeps moving, and finally he is past the row of air conditioners along the building's edge, they and the jackhammer are quiet; he hears the sprinting notes of two birds behind him, and then he is on Gerrard Street. Farther east, there is the yellow font of the Beer Store, and two men walking in tandem toward it; the one on the left clatters a wheeled buggy with grocery bags of bottles to return. He follows, looking up to see the smoke unabated, inking the sky. Beside him, there is a small communal garden started in an abandoned lot: a lumpy blue tarp, and in wooden beds, sprouts of leafy tops, carrots or dill, he can't tell exactly. All of this is semi-obscured by the interlocking chain links of the fence and then the mural bolted to it that runs all the half-dozen metres to the intersection, beginning with two giant bats, one in profile with one large orange eye, another hanging with its wings wrapped around itself; these morph into a herd of bison, the lustre of their coats shining under the noon sun. There are weeds along the underside of the painting and its end, where there is a short man looking toward downtown: he sees this man often, black hair and moustache, with a few items laid out for sale on a riding blanket, a toaster, a paperback copy of *Through Diagnosis, Treatment, and Beyond*, an elegant teapot surrounded by matching blue-and-white dishes. Then the stoplight changes and he leaves the man and his things and crosses north.

The cloud has widened, he notices, and has begun advancing closer, away from the lake and coming north, dragging its dark form toward him. When he sniffs the air, he is aware of a new smell: there are strains of garlic but also a musty fish smell, raw. He exhales, and when he inhales there is that same dusty and rotting scent, but now it's mixed with coffee and then, very distinctly, black pepper. This breath, this cloud, it is intoxicating, and he gulps it into his body.

Before the street light can change to go west, a pair of men rush out, hard hats and bright reflective construction vests: the first motions with his hand for the cars to stop, keeping the traffic from the intersection, then both men station themselves at the opposite sides of the crossing, and he hears the horn of the concrete truck as it backs up.

'Yeah, come this way. Hey, stop!' the man alternates, and as the truck reverses further, and now he has a better view of Gerrard, he sees that the original sidewalks are gone, in the process of being replaced: small stakes jut up around fresh cement, and the street is reduced to only two thin lanes by equipment, a Bobcat, a small road roller, a dump truck piled with rubble. The cement truck is all the way through the intersection, sounding off intermittently until it is overpowered by an ambulance siren. The emergency vehicle screams forward, slows, then the nose of its hood is nearly against the oversized cab; the cement truck's driver backs up further, and the ambulance curves around it, the man directing traffic steps back out of its way, and it turns on its lights and blurs past.

When he follows those red-and-white pulses, he sees that it's pulling into the Health Centre halfway up the block, the south side of the building partially covered by a large violet sign. The ambulance stops in the parking lot next to the small fleet of health buses, mobile clinics that pull up next to the shelters along George Street and Parliament Street. Now all the health buses are parked, and the ambulance, and then another right behind it, and quickly they both swing open their doors and two figures burst from the back of the newly arrived one, carry out a stretcher and place it on the ground; he can see a crumpled body turned on its side away from him, the back exposed where the clothes have burned away. The paramedics return to the vehicle and retrieve another, placing it hurriedly beside the first: this body is relatively untouched except that the top of the head along the hairline has been removed. The image of a burning village, its debris and people scattered under horse hooves and the lively cheers of a war party, invades his mind, the aftermath of a massacre. This scene falls from his mind when another figure comes out of the back, groggily shields its eyes as if stunned by the sunlight, and sits down on the bumper.

He cannot remember crossing the street, but he has, the pepper in his nostrils: he is at the corner of Allan Gardens, swinging his head from the figure on the ambulance's bumper beside the two bodies on the stretchers, back to the smoke cloud bearing down on him. Farther up, a TTC bus parks and opens its doors; the traffic heading south is stopped and now he can see that both lanes on Gerrard have halted as well, all the vehicles frozen, windows down. People begin exiting the bus, walking over the grass and into the park, and he follows down the centre path. On the left, a man in a red ball cap fits his body perfectly along the roots of a tree, resting his back and neck against it, then his arms become roots, the bark grows over his skin and begins to burrow into the ground. *Another hallucination?* This man-tree is a half-dozen metres from a group of men in suits, a Cabbagetown canvas bag between them; they are in the shade and relaxed, lying on their sides, and when he looks back to the tree, he blinks at its normalcy before he hears another voice coming toward him on the path.

'Cops took me, yeah,' says a young man in a red sweatsuit, a bandana across his forehead, his cheeks sweaty. 'Yeah, took me. I don't know why? Because,' and he walks past him toward Sherbourne. On the right are three well-dressed women, an elderly one sitting on her walker and flapping her arms to the sun, her white hair brilliant and radiating out from her; the two younger ones at her feet, inhaling deeply, then they look up at her, their faces smiling and eyes bound to her happily contorting face. 'They are almost here. They are here,' she says to the sky, and the two younger women look at each other with adoration, squeeze their hands together, interlocking fingers.

Beyond them, a film shoot is set up, a generator and lights crowding the small, circular gathering space next to the Conservatory's vibrant garden. He remembers that they often shoot TV and films in the park, a sandwich board announcing an active set, and he can see now the long white trailers parked along the south side of Carlton Street, then a group huddled under a makeshift tent-like structure, pointing at the generator, beyond, and as he follows he can see a false memorial set up, old, as if left out in weather, soggy stuffed animals and faded photos, American flags.

He is pried from this tableau by the sharp crack and hiss of a can opening on the closest bench to him, where three men sit, legs extended to the edge of the path.

'No one will say it, but it has to be,' one says while the other sips a beer, and the can pings his eyes with light. *He looks like Allan, but no. He looks like someone else I grew up with.* Squinting, he sees the can passed to the other man, who responds, 'What else?' as he looks over his shoulder at the wall of dark smoke expanding and pressing forward. The third man is asleep next to them, his legs apart and his arms crossed, head back, a shameless and public sleeping pose.

'Hey, what have you heard?' the man drinking turns to him and asks.

'Yeah, have you heard anything?' the other insists.

'Nothing. My phone stopped working. An earthquake. That's what the TV said.'

'I heard someone say it was a plane that got shot down. The States chased it up here, shot it down. Russian maybe.'

'This isn't the eighties. This ain't Reagan.'

'The fuck it isn't.'

'A fighter plane?'

'Yeah, like, the guy said he saw three planes, two chasing the one, shot it down, then it crashed downtown.'

'That's fucking stupid,' the other man contends, and grabs the beer. 'Fucking stupid. Wasn't no plane.'

'Fuck, yeah. The one plane crashed into the tall tower downtown, then it started coming down. And the Americans were chasing it.'

'Wasn't no plane or no tower.'

'Then what was it?'

'Terrorism.'

'Fuck that. It wasn't no racist bogeyman terrorism.'

'I heard a women say it was a gas explosion,' he adds.

The sleeping man jolts, then relaxes, his mouth open.

'It wasn't no accident. You'll see.'

'Well, it wasn't no terrorist either.'

Behind them, a city garbage truck hops the curb and drives up the path from the other end of the park, over the grass, and meanders through the trees and the people in the shade. After that, it turns left, still refusing the path and instead moving toward the far north side, Carlton Street; it passes a pickup truck with identical paint, both vehicles with City of Toronto colouring and logos, drives past the workers there, neon green vests and a pile of pruned branches around them, and continues until it drops over the curb again and picks up speed, driving down the centre of the street between the lanes and stopped cars. From this vantage he knows he should be able to see the puncturing tip of the CN Tower, the always visible monument, but now it's obscured by ash and dust, and the normal low humming chatter of people in the park is replaced by multiple ambulance sirens. As he listens, he pictures a mouth opening tremendously wide, then shrinking, a mouth in oscillation, *That's how a siren is made.* A man walking by snorts snot loudly, narrowly misses a biker who streaks past him, adjusting at the last second around the man; there is another biker behind that one, no helmet, shirt open, both figures moving fast, bisecting the park, away from downtown.

'You, you don't believe,' the man who had been sleeping mumbles. 'You need teaching.'

'Teaching,' the second man repeats, rising from the bench. The mumbling man gets to his feet as well, sleepwalking, and begins to walk toward him. 'You, you come here, you need to understand!'

As the trio advances, he turns from them and runs in the direction of the white dome of the Conservatory, through the film set and past a light tower, hears a sharp yell from his left, and stumbles over a thick cord, yanking a light toward him. The men are still steadily advancing. He rights himself and, in a panic, bursts through the Conservatory's doors.

He is smacked by the increased humidity inside, a strata of air that he has to slice through, its sediments clinging to him as he enters the Palm House; he bats back a wasp that is flying around his chest, then runs his forehead along the sleeve of his shirt, the sweat settling into his shoulder. There is a ring of a path inside the initial dome where he has entered, and the stones are textured with puddles and divots; the centre of the room is a tiered collection of plants, white and green, then magenta, and then palm trees through those lower levels.

Hurrying, he brushes one as he walks forward, to the left, and his foot echoes off an old metal grate on the floor simultaneous with the light tickle of the plant against his forearm. In his memory, he is suddenly pressed against a tree trunk in the woods; his father is shouting for him, and the thin, spidery branches tickle his wrist as he looks for further cover; his father swaggers out of the shadows then, toward him, large and bowlegged. This image is broken by a tracking shot from the movie last night following horseback riders along a hill's crest, and this is bisected by a voice, 'Excuse me,' as the man slips past him on the path, smelling like pine needles. He moves his eyes, breathing heavy, from the man's back to the strips of sun leading up to the roof, the ringed beams and glass chopping the light and cascading it down in parts, and it is only then that he notices the competing buzz of the lights and the whomp of the fans. The water drips off the plants as the current courses through the building, and a vine slithers out toward his shoe and threatens to climb his leg, to wrap around it and constrict, the hums and the vine, and he startles away and the plant recedes. He inhales quickly, the air expanding droplets in his lungs. *Am I going crazy?*

The trio of men haven't followed, for whatever reason, he thinks, then assures himself that he's not losing his mind, he just needs to think, wait it out, that the building will be safe for a time and then he can sneak by the men and their ambush. He continues, the small letterings beside the plants guiding him – *Ficus lyrata Fiddle-Leaf Fig*, then *Calathea zebrina Prayer Plant* – and he exits to the left, to the offshoot of the dome, the railings on either side making an S-shape down a softly angled ramp, where there are shaggy ferns hanging down the centre as the path splits. A worker sprays the plants: she is wearing blue plastic gloves and coating the plants in water tinged slightly green; the stone is wet around her and she does not turn to see him. She lifts one leaf to inspect as he slides by her, and she pulses the trigger in sweeping motions in front of her – *Russelia equisetiformis Coral Plant, Fatsia japonica Japanese Aralia*. He approaches the koi pond at the junction of the two paths, at the end of this wing of the building. The fish braid around each other, oranges and ghostly whites, tail fins propelling them from one edge of the pond to the other, a swirling mass; they go faster, and the speed makes them blur into a tornado shape, and in its eye is the largest carp, pure and bleached, and the other fish circle it until they are a hurricane. The surface of the water barely ripples, and the centre carp puckers and unpuckers its round mouth, as if mouthing a silent siren sound. He shakes his head in disbelief and the fish slow, return to their normal speeds, darting, diving.

The statue that guards the pond, grey and pocked, is a naked young woman pouring from a jug a quarter her size, her gaze down toward a ruffled swan, its head upturned so that the two are staring at each other. He had been here with Melanie once, days before they broke up: they stood in this same place, looking at the statue, her arm resting on his bicep, a kiss on her forehead. *She seemed happy.* She had explained that the statue was of Leda and the Swan and described the different images of Leda that had manifested across history, the recreated lost da Vinci and Michelangelo paintings. But, she clarified, in Michelangelo's depiction the swan's neck is between the breasts and rising to her mouth, beak and lips in near kiss. Zeus raped her, she explains, the two bodies in impossible contortions, against their biology, and then Leda hatches two children from golden eggs, and he pictures a baby's arm puncturing through the shell, a tiny fist unflexing in the air and coated in snow-coloured membrane, then the other arm, until the child pulls himself through, the head emerging and squalling. Leda takes the child to her still bare breast for comfort while the other shell cracks ominously at her feet, spiderwebbing open. The image of the shell cracking and spread in his mind morphs into the TV image of the burning roof and tower, and he thinks of his windows shuddering, the downtown flames, the smoke and breathing it in, the burning and clouding, his brain repeating, burning and clouding, at the edge of his body and this space. Melanie could be scared or hurt or lost, he insists to himself, he needs to text her, to go over and see her, wedge himself in her doorway and keep out any danger. He brightens his phone screen but there's still no reception, no message from her, but he knows she would want him to reach out, to protect her. *No*, the other side of his mind counters, remembering her upset eyes as she handed him his jacket.

But those men outside, hunting, they're after me, and he moves forward, looking toward the front doors: the path loops back to the domed room, and he starts down. The plants here grow up the walls, gripping the edges and pulling up, a cluster of red bursting flowers dots one rising set of branches, *Weeping Bottle-brush*, purple buddings with thin overlapping leaves, *Liliaceae aspidistra Cast Iron Plant*, then the drooping flowers of bleeding hearts, two bulbings and a white tip. There is a man with an expensive camera around his neck walking with his hands behind his back, and a woman trailing behind him, a teenage daughter even farther back, large expressive eyes, dark hair. She settles on a bench to his left, among the variety of leaves, white with green veins, the pink flowering overlaid over forest green, ferns, spiky long explosions and soft flat curvings. 'Just a bit longer,' the father says to the teenager. Opposite them, a tree, unique among the surrounding palm trees: it is stubby, as if each limb has been systematically cut off, closer and closer to the trunk each year, it has no top, just expands out into its stocky appendages in a star-like motion, and along those outstretches there is a faint moss that hangs down, the sleeves of an oversized robe, as if the tree has tried to slip inside a larger version that lingered only in ornament around it, ghostly over-lay, double trees.

He finds a bench opposite, and as he sits he realizes where he has seen the tree before, or at least some version of it: he was in his final year of high school and in the library gathering books for a report he needed to write on the British Columbia gold rush. He had already read about the other Canadian myths, the Hudson's Bay's inroads, had read about the men on exoduses flowing west, over the Rocky Mountains or up through the Pacific Northwest, across all the unsettled and wild land; he was taught about men who would work those pans on a plot of creek, the water running over the rocks and in rhythm with their optimistic sifting, the boxes and shakers that rose to be storeys tall in order to process the riverbeds faster. He loved to picture those men, striding across nature, claiming anything they could lay their bedroll on, drive their tent pegs into, fighting when someone crossed them; he would play in his backyard at drawing his gun fast enough to ward off someone who was trying to steal his claim, his toy pistol aimed, steady, his legs apart and eyes squinting, before he pulled the trigger.

He had found a photo of the tree in a copy of *British Columbia's World War II Fight* when he was looking for any scraps of his hometown: there were descriptions of the cadet camps along the highway into town, and a few paragraphs on the logging village nearby, casual photos where air raid sirens loomed in the background of a parade, their sentinel speaker perched along the roadside, those same sirens that still stood when he was a child, repurposed to warn of forest fires. He was hoping to find out more about the memorial in the park near his house that listed all the local men who went to fight and died. His father told him that a ranch near their house used to host army training, where cadets would practise scaling walls and dodging mines, sleep in the barracks off the cattle fields. Curious if this was true, he flipped to the book's centre: he didn't see the ranch but instead soldiers piled into chunky trucks, a pilot and his plane, maps showing the exact location of army training sites paired with a number of shots of camps themselves, a collection of long, low blank buildings, set to spy down over the valleys; after this were photos of barbed wire and masses of people behind them, an orderly row of tents in background, and a poster that in block letters said NOTICE TO ALL JAPANESE PERSONS AND PERSONS OF JAPANESE RACIAL ORIGINS. He had seen the tree in a photograph, this mossy tree, the ghostly strings doubling its limbs. In the photo, the same tree, to the right of a Japanese family minus its father, the mother in a swooping hat, bag clutched in front of her, her daughter in a similar white hat and looking directly at the camera, a package neatly crossed with string in her hands and her coat draped over her forearm, her brother the smallest and obscured by suitcases, then further covered by the stack of blankets on top of the luggage, all very orderly, and the caption read, *A family of Japanese Canadians being relocated in British Columbia, 1942*. 'Did you know?' he asked his father that evening. 'Why would they teach you that?' his father answered.

Emerging from his memories, he hears the lights and the fans and now the clicking of a camera, semi-regular shutter snicking, then the bing of a received text, the whoosh of a returned message. He cannot pinpoint the exact sources of these but hears them loudly, across from him *Asplenium nidus Bird's*

Nest Fern, and he takes his phone from his pocket and sees his mother's text first, then Allan posting to their group chat. He logs in and he taps the green icon, reads: *Just wanted to make sure you're okay it looks crazy there.* Switching to his unanswered conversation with Melanie, he types, *Where are you? Everything okay?* and he returns to his mother's texts and types, *I'm fine. I'll call later tonight*, swapping back to Melanie, *I'm coming to you.* He waits for her to answer, swapping to the group chat where Allan has shared articles from his Facebook feed, *Military Responding to Toronto Centre Attacks* and *Antifa claim responsibility for Toronto bombing.* He clicks on the first link, but the page doesn't open; his reception has dropped away again, and he sees that his message to Mel is caught, unsent. Then there is a click of a camera, and when he looks up, the man points his lens directly at him, quickly takes three photos in succession, smiles, then takes two more. 'Hold still,' he says, 'I'm almost done. Very handsome, rugged.' In reaction, he raises his own hand to block his face. 'Hey, what are you doing?' but the man has left, turned out of view. He gets up to find him, sits back, rotates his phone, confirms that there is no signal and puts it back in his pocket, cranes to try to glimpse the camera and the man, *Where did he go?*, then stands up, turning toward the bathroom.

To the right, past the exit that empties eventually into the cacti at the opposite end of the building, he follows the arc of the circle path, *Ficus benghalensis Banyan Tree*, and the bathrooms are off to the side; he turns the corner and enters through their open door, the cloud's peppery coffee smell. The lights are not on, but there is enough from the windows and open door to make the room flicker with light like a projectionist booth. There are urinals and one stall and a man standing at the sink, looking into the mirror, who he tries not to notice. Instead, he pivots away from the man to the porcelain on the left, unbuttoning then unzipping his pants.

'Crazy day, huh?' The stranger's voice echoes off the concrete walls back to him.

'Yeah. Hot too.'

'No, I mean the bombing. Can you believe it?'

'Bombing?'

'Yeah, they fucking blew up a building downtown.'

'Who?'

The man does not respond immediately and, instead, snorts, a pig rooting in the mud for a dismembered finger. Then, when he does speak, the voice is a whisper, directly behind him, on the back of his neck, a soft voice, so close he can feel the light spit of the consonants.

'It's all connected, they connect everything and this is a small part of a larger reckoning, they are just waiting for something like this.' The voice pauses.

He has finished peeing but is frozen, the stranger behind him. The man's body is pulsing heat, its presence enlarging, pinning him against the wall, urgent.

'You'll see.'

Then there is a release and he feels his body being pushed forward, against the tree trunk of his memory again, his father's drunk bellow, then off balance, a shove hard enough to force him to put one hand to the concrete to keep his head from cracking against it; with the other, he frantically tries to keep his pants from falling down, his breath, his pulse, his eyes; he hurriedly rebuttons and zips and turns around. There is no one: it is the same bathroom he entered, with the exception of a pile of fabric. It's misshapen by the bulky object inside, and he is cautious, approaches; it is a grey cavalry coat, and when he unfolds it he sees the original colours are stained over by a rusty brown splotching. Then he sees the edges of an object that the jacket is wrapped around, a sabre, long and antique, ornamented by liquid, fresh and glistening.

He throws the bundle against the wall, bounds out and around the circle path down the right side, past the entrance to the S-ramp and Leda, and down the small entrance hallway until he is outside. *The gun. Home. The gun.* The sunlight contracts his vision, and the whole park begins to implode, pulling impossibly fast to a hard, dense centre, a black hole; blindly, he walks forward then south, down the wide shallow steps, his eyes are closed and he is walking quickly with panicked instinct, feels the concrete change to lawn, and sinks, legs under him and knees on the grass, his hands down and bracing, and he stays like this, heaving.

With his eyes closed, he begins to calm himself by listening, tries to orient himself by identifying the layers of noise that are always present in a city, but he doesn't hear anything but a faraway siren. No conversations, no birds, no traffic, no construction noises; it is as if the world has been emptied. He cracks open his eyes and swings his head around, sees no one, the cars on Gerrard are parked and abandoned; the three men are gone as if they had never been there. There are no pedestrians, just the plastic bags and makeshift tents left under trees; there are no bodies lying on their sides in the grass, no one propped up on the benches. Maybe the world has been emptied, he considers. There is just the heat and the silence.

His breath grows shallower, his movement to his feet spastic. He shuts his eyes again and takes three steps forward. There is sound again, slowly fading back up; he can hear it through the slats of his fingers, a woman yells, then the brakes of a large vehicle shush and a diesel engine idles, there are footsteps and the chunky irregular clanging of a shopping cart being pushed over uneven ground, and his eyelids lift and the world is repopulated. When he pivots his gaze, however, everyone he can see has stopped what they were doing, nervously glancing at each other, caught in a tension hunched on the edge of fleeing.

He breaks this by crosscutting rapidly across the grass of the park, to Gerrard Street, habitually looks both ways, then twists through the cars and construction equipment, over the half-finished road, the black asphalt dry and unmarked, the texture of lava. He is galloping across, down George Street, trying to summon the image of a cowboy riding hard into the teeth of the enemy attack. Empty tall recycling bins are thrown haphazardly onto the sidewalk and he warps himself around these obstacles, a blue porta-potty with a yellow roof, the door with a slice of red, locked, *Occupied*. There is a trailer that holds sheaths of plywood, and past this there is a closed shipping crate, its door barred and its outer wall graffitied, FOR LIFE KID LION the only clear lettering among the looping tags, and he moves fast by all this, trying to outdistance the coat, the sabre, the seductive voice in his ear, pressed against him, explaining.

Across the street is a black iron fence surrounding picnic tables, a long building cut evenly by three horizontal rows of windows. People glare at him as he passes the building, the entrance sign: HOSTEL *Emergency Shelter and Administrator, Long Term and Annex Harm Reduction Program's Entrance*, the City of Toronto logo in the right corner, *We are here to* HELP. There is a man on a bike pedalling himself in a languid figure eight, an unnerving non-speed, looping in an infinity shape, and there is a volume of voices. He tries to outwalk their parallel dialogues.

'– another attack. Just now, I felt it, how did you not feel it? It was –'

'– and she was there, Ellie saw the building, saw it go over top of her, she said she saw it –'

'– at war, been at war so long –'

'– drives down from the coast, probably a five-hour drive. Gets to their house. They are all preparing for the wedding–'

'– didn't hit her. I swear I didn't but –'

'– for years for years we've been over there at war –'

'– didn't feel anything, man, a building downtown fucking blew up –'

'– she said it was so low, she could see the landing gear –'

'– there only be one attack? Only one? Look at all that smoke, why is there two –'

'– literally the whole globe on fire. It wasn't just jocks or nerds or Black kids –'

'– saw a truck, though, not a plane, pull past and turn the corner and next thing he knew –'

'– always. Always. We can't not be –'

The housing on the right side of the street, as he walks, gives away to a fenced-off lot, discarded foam coffee cups, a horse's reins, a tube of bright lipstick. This is next to a makeshift memorial, *Rest in Peace Marion Morrison* on white posterboard, a heart with a jagged crack through its centre, bouquets of flowers attached to a balloon in front of the sign; the flowers are pink roses, and two steps farther, he looks up to see four packages of cheese, still sealed, drooped over the top, the consistency barely contained in their plastic. *Filth.* For a moment he is gagging, imagining the texture of the runny cheese barrelling down his throat, back up into his nostrils, the smell of blood on fabric and the glint of metal under bathroom lights, acrid chemical smoke in his lungs, and he involuntarily zags across the street and sags against the chain-link fence there.

'Hey, stop that!' A security guard, a grey uniform with blue trim, gleaming boots, reaches for his walkie-talkie; there is fresh stubble on his cheeks and a holster on his hip. The guard repeats himself, ambling forward, then speaks directly into his walkie-talkie. 'No, it's okay, just some guy,' and a staticky voice squawks unintelligibly in return. 'Yeah. Yeah,' and the guard turns his back, begins to leave, and as he does, he says Melanie's full name into the walkie-talkie.

'What?'

'Just keep moving.'

'How do you know her name?'

'Man, I don't know your name, her name, whoever she is. Just keep moving. Can't be here.'

As he cautiously walks forward down the block, he balances the rising swell of anxiety in his stomach with attention to the senses flooding him. The chain-link fence he is leaning against is protecting a shuttered square home, a former boarding house, he guesses, symmetrical and cresting with a central peak where a small door, boarded up, leads to a shallow balcony; the wood over the windows and doors is lighter than the dark brown of the building, the colour of the grass surrounding the mound of brick and rubble that lies next to it. There is a sign that explains this wreckage, a blue banner and white headline, *Proposal for New Site*, with the scrawl of *Civilization* underneath it in black felt-tip pen, then diagrams, a listing for the number of beds and rooms the project will provide. He watches the guard turn the corner down the alley to the side of the last building. He thinks of the guard's holster, of the Conservatory bathroom, and considers how defenceless he is. Then he remembers his father telling him about the only time he visited Toronto: they were downstairs, sweaty from hitting the heavy bag, and his father explained that as a young man he had been drawn to Yonge Street by the neon facades he saw in photos. He went into one of the strip clubs – 'And you can too when you get old enough,' his father assured him with a wink – and drank beer until late. In the alley, just after closing, a man tried to mug him, 'And I fought him off. He didn't know I had a right cross like that,' and he put himself in his father's eyes, watching the man flee from him, safe in his own defence.

Moving faster, he passes more houses, toward an intermittent set of screeching noises, near Dundas West, passing the back of the Filmore Hotel, *Afternoon Delight 2:00–4:00, European Style Dancing*. Opposite the hotel is a demolition site; there is a gigantic crane, with a bucket at its end, and its teeth grab and pull down a whole floor as he watches, the screech, then a crash that is the simultaneous collection of many sounds, wood on wood, machine, metal, plastic, insulation, motors, and the crane rears again and slices through another former room, the remains, the skeleton, of the building is fuzzy with wires and cables along its edges, and the sun comes harshly through the bones. They are replacing, upgrading; these thoughts seem to attack him from outside his body. When he looks into the yard, he sees all the other machinery is at rest; the gas generator does not chug, the small backhoe is still, the only other engine running, unattended, is one he's never seen before, a bulbous cylinder that looks to be blowing mist: the particles around it roil and crimp but never disappear, like the childhood game of finding shapes in clouds. Within the mist, he sees a cantering horse, a feather, a swan at full wingspan, a fist; beyond is the gradually sloped funnel of dark smoke downtown. The cloud is denser and its edges are starkly black against the sky, a deep-bottomed hole against the heat-hazy backdrop, incrementally growing wider, closer, as he rounds the corner to the block his apartment is on.

The sidewalk in front of Filmore's is busier than it was before, a horde that spooks when a heavy object is dropped at the construction site, a clang then an earthy thump; they turn toward the sound, briefly, then back, and he cuts through them briskly. The crowd seems to tighten around him as he tries to go against the tide of their downtown gaze. He leaves the sidewalk and walks in the road, walking past a blue sedan with an empty baby seat in the back; the next silver car has a pair of shoes under the steering wheel, as if the person had been lifted cleanly out.

Recrossing Pembroke, he makes a diagonal to the doors to his building. As he takes out his keys and opens the door, he pauses to make sure no one is following him. There is a candy wrapper just inside that flutters and glints in the low light, and its flickering movements trigger the memories of the whisper in his ear, the drip of red off the sabre's blade. Breathing quickly, he takes the stairs two at a time, can feel his chest fill, the air expanding, bigger, his breath harsh in its exhale, reaches the second-floor landing. Someone has written ETHAN on the walls here, and his breath is even more ragged as he blurs past the third storey, his footsteps the only echo; he looks up, the sequenced rising of each floor spiralling up, he thinks of the inside of an impossibly large smokestack, that he is rising as smoke rises, then finds the fourth floor without pausing, and is in the hallway. *I need to get to her, protect her, there is danger all over*, he shouts to himself. At a near jog with keys in hands before he reaches, turns the knob, and is inside, finally stopping with his back against his thin door.

He does not take his shoes off, ignores his small kitchen and the unwashed dishes in the sink, houseflies resting on the cutlery; he nearly trips on the empty beer bottles from the night before, grouped together. He goes past the closet to his immediate right, his TV's blank face, his hand-me-down plaid couch, the empty walls marked only by the grime of his hands on the corners where he often grips drunkenly in the dark, navigating late at night. The door to his bathroom is slightly open, but he turns the other direction into his bedroom, sensing the presence of someone in his apartment.

'Hello?'

The voice that answers starts as a familiar low drawl, but the last few words glitch into a computer sound, reminding him of a DVD stuttering. 'It's me. I let myself in.'

He recoils into the kitchen and waits, thinking of the steak knife in the drawer the minute he hears movement. But after a minute of nothing, he steps tentatively toward his bedroom, his fists by his side. A wave of anger rises in him, as he imagines someone going through his space, his home. He notices then the thrill of this fury; he is not scared but rather ready, incensed, champing and straining forward, and he pushes hard against the bedroom door, throwing it open.

He doesn't remember having left the window open, but it is, *The cloud is in here now,* and the breeze that runs to him reminds him how hot his apartment is without an air conditioner. *No one,* he assures himself, but the adrenaline remains, his muscles alert and wanting. The bed is under the window and there are piles of clothes around it, jeans and balled socks, it is all he can smell, the sweat of the past days' heat and alcohol, and he is sweating now as he kneels in front of his dresser and pulls the bottom drawer with both hands, sorting through track pants, a shirt from a childhood basketball camp, one dress sock. Underneath, at the back, his hand finds it, the weight and metal of it, and he pauses and feels it first in his grip, then bounces it in his flat palm.

He stands and walks back out of the room, his arm and the handgun dangling by his side. He raises it quickly to shoulder height and looks down its barrel; he can feel his father's steadying hand on his upper arm. 'Hold it. Don't fire yet, hold it. Hold it until you don't feel it'; his father explained that he must wait until the gun felt like an extension of his fingers and palms, arm, and held no weight at all. 'You never know when you might need protection': his father always repeated the phrase, even the last time he saw him, his voice a shell of his commanding low rumble, from his hospital bed, oxygen tanks, the cancer stampeding through him, the tubes snaking from his arms and mouth, the monitors blinking reds and numbers against the antiseptic whites of the room.

When he sits down, he places the gun on the coffee table, grey and black and sleek, pointing the barrel toward the TV and away from him. 'Never point it at yourself or anyone you don't want to shoot,' his father told him as he handed it to him. 'You can never be too careful.' He had lied to Melanie: he had taken the gun out after she broke up with him and sat on the couch of his old apartment, the gun on the coffee table, much like it is now. But that evening had passed, and he had made no movement toward the gun and the outside world. The next morning he put it away, though he thought of it occasionally, and of that night. After he had moved into this apartment, he placed it in the bottom drawer, where it sat, unfired, until he retrieved it just now; he had thought of it often in the first weeks of living in the city, as the shouts and sirens rose up to him in the dark – 'Just to be safe,' his father would repeat. 'You just never know.'

When he drags his eyes to his router he sees his Wi-Fi is working, and he leans back on the couch and pulls out his phone: no reception. However, his prior text from Allan Gardens had finally gone through, and his mother has responded, *Glad to hear you're okay we are so scared, are you going to come home?, Come home please, where it is safe, it is not safe there, Terrorists, there are terrorists in your city*. He replies, *I'm going over to Melanie's now, and will call from there, when both are safe, no not coming home, not yet. Don't worry I'm safe.* He taps to the text conversation with Melanie, adds to his last response, *You must be terrified. I'm coming over, don't worry*, then switches over to his Twitter, #Torontoriots, and the news accounts that populate the top of his feed have shifted their information, *Firefighters try to contain fire, Chaos on the streets around Toronto event, Toronto police advise people to not leave their homes.* He scrolls down and sees personal feeds: the first shows a picture of a group huddled outside a smashed shop window, captioned with *Riots in my neighbourhood! #LittleItaly*; another: *Someone is opening and closing all the doors in my apartment building and slamming them, so scared*; another: *There is a dead police horse outside on the sidewalk, they say they are coming but too busy to do anything soon*; then, a photo of a car on fire in the middle of the street and two blurred figures fleeing from it, identical black cloths pulled up over their mouths like bandits. His mind is back in the Conservatory bathroom – 'You'll see,' the whisper voice and the smell of piss, the moulting fabric wrapping that dark, wet sabre. He adds to his message, *Mel Fuck it's crazy out there. I will be there as soon as I can, don't worry. I'll be there soon.* I can't let her be alone, he thinks as he sends the text. *She has no one else. Only me.* He mentally maps out the route: he can be at her door in forty-five minutes if he cuts straight across the city.

He grabs the gun and goes back to the bedroom, to the bottom drawer again, and finds the ammunition; after he slides the magazine from the handle, he presses the bullets in one by one, then reinserts the magazine firmly. The movie from last night returns in his mind: John Wayne, after hunting for two years, returns, dirty and weary but proud, leaves as soon as he gets the scrap of the girl's dress, into the silent morning, while the rest of the world is still and unknowing and frightened.

He clicks the safety on and slides the gun into the waistband of his pants, undoing his belt quickly, then tightening it to better hold the weapon in place, before dropping his shirt over it; he wiggles to test it and, satisfied, checks his back pocket for his wallet, gets his keys back in his hand.

There is a complete vacuum of noise in the hallway as he steps out: there are no TVs or radios or voices through the thin walls; all of it is quiet as he locks his door. As he walks down the flattened carpet of the hallway, he suspects that those left in the building are either looking out the windows that face the city centre or pressed against their own doors, maybe with a chair protectively wedged under the knob. If they did look out, fish-eyed, he would look bowlegged, his torso and head enlarged and immediate, his whole body warped larger, formidable.

He blurs through the stairwell, the three floors down, the lobby and door. He exits out onto the sidewalk, and the smell in the air has shifted from its early peppery tinge to must, like an old book being opened, mixed with the heavy exhaust of dozens of trucks moving in convoy. His arms and hands lightly brush people as he walks past the dry cleaner, the convenience store, the Bar and Grill, and only now registers the green storefront across as there is a woman knocking heavily on the closed entrance, a large advertisement for sugarcane juice, two ATM signs in red bolding, and the back of an air conditioner unit extruding directly above the woman now pounding.

'Hey, come out!' Her white tank top is yellowed at the waist where it bunches sweatily. The paint on her toenails is chipped and hot pink.

Another man comes up beside her. 'Open up!' He points to the awning above them, green with white symbols, *ge'ez abugida, Paissa Injera and Takeout*, and the man begins pounding, shaking dust from the bars across the window, motes around his fists. A cracked sign below reads *The Best Espresso in the World*, and the strangers hit the window with the flats of their hands, 'Open up!' The men across the street, beers warm, wait, and the flow of people in dusted business clothing, mouths and noses covered, regains momentum, their footsteps leaving remnants of powder as they pour around the stalled streetcar, the pay phone, the intersection.

'We wanna see you all,' the woman says. 'We know. We know.'

'We know!' the man adds, and picks up a rock, weighing it in his hand, then warning the woman: 'Look out.'

She steps back, and he hurls it through the top window, just above where the bars end, piercing into the shop; the clatter of its landing mixes with a siren blocks away, and the man bends at the waist, looking for another potential projectile.

'Don't,' he hears himself say. He imagines Mel's admiring gaze as the camera of his mind's eye pans across from the pair to himself, and he can see himself standing with legs firmly planted, his back straight, commanding, then the camera pushes in on the gun in his waistband.

'What?' The man moves to a chest-high recycling bin and opens the lid. 'Don't what?' He starts to reach in, then simply topples it over: the guts of it spill out, entrails of soda and beer leak from unfinished cans and bottles rolling onto the sidewalk, sheets of discarded faxes with vacation deals, a single boot with spurs at the heel, a grocery-store flyer livid with staged food photos swirl around his feet as he kicks them aside, searching. 'Don't what?'

The woman sifts through the tipped-out contents with him, dropping to one knee. She looks up, 'We just know.'

'Stop. Just go.' He keeps his tone even, inflecting it with stoic hardness. Admiring his own voice, he reaches his hand across his stomach. The woman follows this gesture, sees the gun, hitches to her feet. He sees something in her panic, an assurance that she has had someone threaten her in this way before, perhaps often.

'We … It's okay. We'll go. Come on.' She grabs the man's arm.

'What the fuck?' The man backs away with her, and seeing his posture, legs apart, rigid, hand across his body and along his waistband, he challenges, 'Fuck you.' He notices the smear of takeout food on their hands and feet, grains of rice sticky between toes, some sauce or dirt, ochre between knuckles, as he gestures with his head for them to go up Pembroke, to leave. As he returns his hand, the musty smell he noticed when he first left his building becomes tinged with smoke; the breeze blowing from downtown, against his face, cools him momentarily.

'Just go.'

'Okay, okay. But we know,' she says, dragging the man. He watches them go north, their heads systematically turning back to look at him, and he lets them get a half block away before he pivots. Feeling the stares of the men outside the Bar and Grill, their eyes dragging down to his waistband, the bulge there, then back up, he grins, a lopsided curl of his lips at the crowd. None of their facial expressions change, each a frozen grimace against him, the bottles in their hands forgotten in their interrogation.

'Boy, get rid of that.' He's seen the man before, out front past midnight, laughing, a hand resting on the shoulder of another man as they keel slightly. Now he has a dark blue shirt on, a security firm with a red-eyed eagle on a shoulder patch, and he repeats his warning without moving.

'I'm going. I have to go.' He retreats, and another man across the street, south side, hollers a name, 'Jamie,' maybe 'Valerie.' When the man in blue turns to assess, he moves quickly away from them, against the tide and toward Filmore's, away from the shouting, which sounds more like 'Melanie' the farther he moves away. He thinks sharply: the memory of her kitchen, pouring bourbon into their glasses; he could hear her in the other room, looking for books, shifting on shelves, crouching, and when he returned, she straightened up, turning to him, back to the couch. 'We had some good times. We were younger then too.' When he had entered the apartment, his first thought was that she had grown smaller and more delicate than he remembered; on the couch, she seemed even more so, with the living room growing large around her, leaning inward, as if mountains, as if tall pines in a night forest. The revelation of her vulnerability, captured from her kitchen door frame, jerks him into the present and his urge to move toward her now is swelling, shielding.

A person runs into him, hard, stumbles, then is on their feet; he is jarred, grabs for his own shoulder, a bruise rising as he continues in the opposite direction from the steady, hurried-eastward mass that covers the street. The cloud has advanced, he notices, now a creep, but insistent and ever-present. He steps briskly by a parking lot, mostly full, the asphalt webbed and aged around the edges, cylindrical traffic cones, orange and black, marking the parking spaces. There is a smell, a liquid odour, heat fermented and assaultive. Just beyond, leaning against the far side of the white shed, a man watches him; he's smoking, the haze obscuring, but he can see his jeans, his thumbs hooked into the belt loops, muscles underneath the white V-neck, a long inhale, then he flicks the butt to the ground.

Both of their heads swivel to the northwest corner of the lot when they hear a shout: they both see an open sedan trunk, ten metres away, a suitcase on its side, bright clothes on the ground, and a man is throwing objects to either side of him, too far away for exact details but he hears a small electronic device bounce and crack dramatically. 'Fuck!' the stranger yells again, and dives back into the car. He stalks toward this stranger, who removes himself from the car and straightens, jogs to the next car and rears back his arm, a tire iron, smashing it forward into the window, shattering it, followed by a car alarm jumping.

'Hey!' He surges at the man, and his mind's camera follows him as he strides. The alarm whoop yawns around him as he approaches, in time to see the stranger find a wire underneath the steering wheel, yank, and the noise halts, replaced by the babble of the street behind him, helicopter blades speeding overhead. He pulls up as the stranger picks up the tire iron. A birthmark runs the lower part of the man's right chin, the colour of muted war paint; he is wearing something around his neck, gilded and four-armed. His mouth stretches into a near-smile as he takes one firm step toward him: the two across from each other, his own chest sticking to his shirt, and his hand through his hair, a heavy exhale catching his breath, and the stranger advances. He retreats one step and can feel the gun slip slightly down his leg, loosened from the jog over; it is digging into his pelvis, the barrel warm through his underwear, and he adjusts it. As he does, the stranger lunges, barely missing. He reverses, stumbling at his waistband.

'Okay, look, whoa.'

'Just fuck off!' The stranger comes toward him, relentless.

'I'm going, I'm going.' He backs away, adjusting the gun haphazardly, as it threatens to slide farther down his leg.

The stranger points with the tire iron. 'Fuck off.' His feathered green eyes are set into a handsome face, stubble, striking jawline.

'Okay, okay, I'll go, I'll go.'

Backing away, he is on the sidewalk, pivoting into the crowd, looking back to see the stranger is out of sight. He cuts in front of a woman moving south, shouldering and wedging between other people, until he nearly stumbles over a person kneeling on the street, raising a child above her, a young blond boy. They are in the middle of the street while other people move around them, a rock in moving water. He stops, bends to one knee next to them, and the voice, neither masculine nor feminine, is a desperate whisper, then a slithering mutter; the child is eerily calm, entranced, looking straight into the sky. The person speaks: 'And if it collapses, when it collapses, he will, they will, in Heaven, who art watching, always watching except when they aren't, she will but then and over and over again. There is a, there is a place where we will all, afterward if belief, in believing we must, and only in rising can they meet,' and then he is jostled over, his hands on the hot pavement to steady himself, his leg bent awkwardly underneath him; he crawls on all fours, shoes past and around him, to one knee, then stands. He lurches past the kneeling figure, the boy, and onto the opposite sidewalk.

There, on the south side of the street, is a large pit, the foundation of a building under construction, and he steps around those passing by him, then rests by hooking his fingers into the chain-link fence barricading the pit off from the public. He moves past the two cement trucks churning, their mesmerizing rotation, past the row of porta-potties, and then he sees it: the cloud has grown larger, darker, oddly smelling of fresh plants like cut hay and cow corn, like the fields from his childhood, with the slight linger of bleach, edges tinged with a shimmer of cobalt, emerald, goldenrod, the colours of a vista sunset. He can see it has drawn nearer, understands that if it keeps expanding as it is, it threatens to wrap itself around the glass pillar building at the intersection within the hour, swallow it. He imagines its texture, a new sensation for him: he can feel it enter his nostrils, his open mouth and down his throat, vapour into his lungs; he imagines himself full, completely filled, swollen on the verge of bursting. The only way he can break this image from his consciousness is to imagine it leaving his body, leaking from his pores, the smoke rising off his skin and into the air, an aura, gunmetal, slate, ash, falling to his feet as silt and dust. In this vision, his exhale vibrates, a deep low note in his organs that blooms from him, shudders the ground, followed by a mechanical-sounding inhale, metal on metal, scraping, screeching, then out, and as he breathes, he becomes towering, commanding. As he grows, the note shifts, muffled slightly but lower, menacing, and unmistakably the sound of hundreds of horse hooves pummelling the earth; the noise changes again and its drone deepens and he remembers the tire iron pointing at him, the stranger mocking his paralysis and weakness. Now the noise vibrates at a frantic frequency, distant unpausing gunshots, making him nauseated, passing into his intestines, into his blood, the cloud circulating through his entire body.

He nearly trips in his hurry to escape this vision, to the southwest corner of Dundas and George, where he stops, heaving.

The sound has stopped abruptly, the interiors of his body settling as he tries to reorient himself, looking first at Filmore's across the street, then down George Street toward the lake. He pulls his phone from his pocket, sees there is no network, no response from Melanie. Frantic, he tries airplane mode to reset the data as he imagines her huddled in her bed, scrolling through her Facebook feed, her Twitter, typing, *Please come please*, but the message can't get to him; she can't look out the window, he thinks, it's too much, and so she is barricading herself in the bedroom.

'You getting anything?' one of the women across the street hollers at him, interrupting his fantasy.

'What?'

'You getting anything?' She waves him over to two other young women in front of Filmore's, all in their mid-twenties, backpacks at their feet. She shouts over the thinning crowd of people leaving downtown, and he starts to weave casually through to them, stuffing the phone back into his pants. When he reaches them, he makes eye contact with each one, all three are young and attractive: a Black woman with her hair tied back, the second with waterfall blond hair just past her shoulders, hand above her large round eyes behind large black frames, the third, the one who waved him over and speaks with a slight Pakistani lilt, slight shoulders and arms.

'Sorry, we can't get any reception. We are trying to call our parents. Or anyone.'

'No. Nothing either. Well, sort of. It has been cutting in and out. I keep getting messages but I can't respond.'

'This is so unreal.'

'I'm sorry,' he offers. 'I'm trying to get across town. To a friend. She's terrified.'

'Oh wow, good luck.'

'Yeah, good luck. We just came from class, Katherine and I. And in the middle, someone says, "Holy shit," and everyone pulls out their phones and something has happened.'

'No one knew anything, it just looked wild. So the professor tried going on with the class but people were getting up, leaving the class, coming back. Phones kept ringing, buzzing. The professor stopped the class and we talked about it. She pulled up her own Twitter, and we watched people's feeds and talked and guessed.'

'Oh god, did you see that one guy? He always comes in late, near the back.'

'What did he say? Something about a reckoning, a black pill.'

'Yeah, something about it finally happening. The gentlemen are coming. A hard rain, finally.'

'And that other guy, the one next to him, says something, a word I don't know, it sounded familiar, but he said it in a pissed-off way, then they both laughed.'

'Those guys always creeped me out. Sometimes they stare at you.'

'They don't! Why didn't you tell me.'

'They're too creepy.'

'Anyways, we didn't really think, I guess. We just started following everyone in this direction. I think maybe we thought the reception might get better once we got farther away.'

'We tried the Wi-Fi, but it was out too at the school, and then the power cut out as we were leaving. All the hallways just went dark.'

'And I met up with them when they were walking.' The third woman coughs into her elbow. 'I was sitting on the curb and you asked if I was okay. I think I would still be there if you hadn't asked.'

'Are you feeling any better?'

'Yes. A bit.' She smiles at the first woman, then turns to him. 'I was at Union Station, heading north. I live near St. Clair West Station, so I usually just get on and go all the way south and around to get to campus. We had just got past Union and the train stopped. But not stopped, like, regular. I mean we've all been on trains when they stop, and it sort of jerks and starts and stops. But this was like someone slammed on the brakes. The subways stopped hard, then the lights cut entirely out.'

'Oh god.'

'And I could hear breathing, then people muttering, then a scream. I couldn't see anything. And then I felt hands on me. Two different sets of hands in the dark, one around my waist, the other, fuck, groping me, one trying to unbutton my pants, and I tried to run away, but I bumped into someone else. The hands, pitch black, but then I fell over trying to run away. The emergency lights, I think they were the emergency lights, they came on. There was barely any light, but I could at least see, and there were two shadows walking away. I couldn't see them totally, but it was two pretty big guys.'

'What did you do?'

'I ran the other way, to another car where there was more light, and found a seat. Maybe a minute later, the doors opened. No announcement. And I could see out the doors that there were strings of lights along the tracks and the subway walls. I could still hear people muttering. I was fucking terrified, looking for those guys, hoping they wouldn't find me. Then the conductor, are they called conductors? Anyways, he comes down telling people to get out, get into the tunnel. It was so hot, and the footsteps, it was so creepy how they echoed. I remember keeping one hand along the wall, and I was following an older woman, maybe she was seventy, and she had to move so gingerly, people were passing her, but I don't know, I didn't want her to be alone or I didn't want to, so I just followed her.'

'How long were you down there?'

'I have no idea. We walked and, you know, we would get to a station, like King, but there were already police. I think they were police. They had these huge rifles and they were telling us to keep going. We weren't allowed to leave, and they were yelling for us to move. We would come to another subway car and have to go around. I started holding the woman's hand. Everyone else was way ahead then and it was almost like we were alone, until Queen Station, where we saw the police again.'

'Do you think they might have been soldiers?'

'Oh god, yes, maybe? They did look like in the movies. You know, like army uniform or something. Big guns.'

'Fuck.'

'So we get to Dundas and there are ladders and people helping other people up to the platform. More soldiers. One guy was nice. He asked if I was okay and gave me this bottle of water. But the light was so bright when I got outside, I just sort of stumbled, carried away with everyone else, until I sat down. I wonder where that old woman went.'

The blond woman wraps her arms around her.

'I just hope she's okay. I don't know why I didn't make sure. I just left her.'

'I think I'm going to keep going.' He sees the two women embracing, the third rubbing the crying one in slow large circles on her back. 'My friend, she needs me.'

'We're going to walk a bit more eventually, when she's all right. It'll be okay. I have a friend in Cabbagetown. We'll try to get reception and go there. It should be okay there.'

'Be careful.'

'You too.'

He hears the woman sobbing and gasping as he strides across George Street, westward toward Melanie, past the demolition site again. At the corner there is a blaring *Danger Due To Excavation* sign on a tall chain-link fence: he sees the old Ramada Inn, the skeleton of the building hanging half eaten, in shreds, the beams of the roof exposed; the bottom half looks as if it's been sunk underwater for decades, a grave half filled, or half dug, decayed and mouldy. The former rooms are recognizable, but the floors are covered in plaster, fraying wires swinging casually. A large backhoe is digging at the tall parts of the building, an arm flexing and pulling, its bucket hooked and slowly dragging down parts of the husk. Behind the crane is a scrim of protective netting, and on the ground are two people with hoses spraying into the air, soaking the dust from any chunk that falls to the ground.

Passing under scaffolding, he dips into shade, the sensation settling coolly over his skin, as his eyes adjust to the dark, to the posters lined alongside ads for upcoming albums, movie posters, *Rio Grande, Stagecoach, In Select Theatres*. He reads as he walks: *The Quiet Man, The Man Who Shot Liberty Valance, The Horse Soldiers*. There is a poster with two men on horseback, John Wayne taller than the other, as they ride against an apocalyptically bright sunset, the clouds painted across the sky behind them like the streaks of fighter jets. It sounds like footsteps above him on the scaffolding, walking in exact sync with his own, matching so precisely he's not sure if it's an echo. He pauses, and the steps stop; they begin again when he surges ahead, walking quickly, the gun digging into his pelvis. The light through the scaffolding is light through branches, dappling his face as he speeds ahead.

He approaches the Dundas-Jarvis intersection and sees a smattering of people walking away from the downtown core, hunched but without panic. Looking backward, he notices that the demolished building still has the Ramada facade on the front, and underneath, the lobby is still oddly intact, as if it were checking in guests. He squints and sees the leafy fake plants just behind the chained-closed door, the outline of a hulking desk beyond that, then scraps of light, hinting at its hollowness. There is a development notice on the gate to the left: *A change is proposed for this site*, blue-and-white City of Toronto, 3-1-1, *41 storeys, Public Meeting* and overtop ALL DAY in small caps, then a larger *you fuck ass* in a different hand, then another thick black spray paint cursive *Never*, the 'N' bulbous and the 'r' slashing downward.

'Help! Help me!'

He hears it muffled through walls, female, in a tone that implies the person is acting, as if it were a movie playing in another room, unmistakably from inside the building. *Is that real?*, and he remembers the other instances of his imagination, possible hallucinations despite their vividness, each a type of vision made of smoke. Then he hears the voice again and it's more sincere. 'Please! I'm sorry!' He makes a gap by pulling the gate apart. The voice is familiar: as he moves cautiously he considers the text messages on his phone again, the image of Melanie hiding and waiting for him; this time at her door frame, he sees her look out, one sea-green eye through her cracked door held by the safety chain, then a half smile, and she moves to let him in. His imagination is interrupted by a shout, deep, then a short scream, and he instinctively pries at the gate, wedging it open, then slipping through until the gun hitches on the pole. He reaches behind under his shirt and pulls it out, extended arm holding it as he slides the last bit of his himself past the gate.

He can now see a security company's sign next to the lobby's door, a stylized eagle hunting above block-lettered LIVE PATROL, then *This site is secured and remotely monitored.* Without pausing, he pulls the locked glass door, another shout, rears back and smashes the butt of the gun against the window, once, twice; on the third jarring he cracks through the front, again, once more, and then there is a hole he can reach through, careful of the jagged edges, and turns the horizontal interior lock vertical, pushing the door in. Now that he is closer, he sees that the plants, the desk, the floor are covered in dust, and there are footprints tracked over the floor, wide cowboy boots with deep tread, and there is a sledgehammer in the corner, beside a toolbox and a radio on its side. There is music from somewhere in the room, a soft and inoffensive score, and he follows a long dragged trail through the dirt toward a hallway behind the desk, past a broken mirror, smeared by a gloved handprint.

Then he hears the voice again – 'No!' – and dives ahead. The hallway is long, dozens of identical doors lining each side, and he starts to jog, the gun gripped in his fist; he goes right, down a hallway, as he hears the sharp bark of a man, then something hitting a wall, shaking particles from the ceiling. The numbers on the door stream by him, then a left turn to another hallway, the dark carpet cushioning his shoes as he accelerates, left again, and there is a small exit sign above a stairwell. He's near certain the voice is coming from at least one floor up, and this is confirmed when there is a stomp, then the sound of hundreds of pounds being dropped. Instinctually, he is pushing through the door, up the concrete steps that turn as he ascends, to the small plateau and then out into another hallway, the mirrored replica of the floor below. He runs, turns, turns again: he listens for more noise, but the closed doors don't offer any hints. He is jolted by the sharp breaking of wood, the snap followed by a close-by shattering. He swings himself around another corner into a new space, rows of doors and one near the end is open, splinters at its frame. As he gets closer he can smell food, greasy chicken and something that mixes garlic and fried onions, slows as he approaches, creeping forward, the gun held in front of him, his eyes down its barrel, his hand supporting his wrist and his finger curling around the trigger, sliding the safety off, his father's hand on his own as he chambers a round and backs against the wall outside the door, listens.

Nothing.

He strains for any sort of movement, any small tick of bodies in the room, but can only hear the far-off sound of the crane digging into the building. He remembers being in the forest with his father, his senses rising to the challenge of tracking a deer through the underbrush, gathering the smallest signs: a broken end of a branch, an indent in the soft earth. But there is the other memory: hiding behind the widest tree trunk he can find, his father shouting his name, louder as he hears his boots get closer. The snapping of twigs underfoot fills him as he returns to the present; he leads with the gun as he bursts forward, enters, surveying the empty space, the bathroom door gone, and the sink taken, the gaping pipes underneath, wiring spilling from where the light fixtures used to be.

'Who's there?' he demands, peering, the sunlight through the windows exposing the hairline cracks that cover each wall, slithering into the patchy floor. There is a grocery bag pushed against the baseboard by his feet, and he steps further inside, drawn to the window. He looks out, blood slowing, and notices that there is almost no one on Dundas Street now; he looks south down Jarvis, which is nearly abandoned. There is the combination of the sun stabbing off the glass of the new condo at the opposite corner, but he can also make out the reflection of the expanding downtown smoke, now darkened beyond colour, now deep thunderhead black, threatening the most vicious storm and fury, and the effect disorients him.

He doesn't feel the punch to the back of his head, but it bends his knees, and he nearly drops the gun, manages to half spin with his arm flying out in front of him, a fist slicing air, and he backs against the far wall, raising his weapon. The man dodges, weaves, then lunges forward. The smell is now mouldy hay, mud, and when he pulls the trigger, the man yells, the shot and his voice echoing in the small space, and his ears are bursting and his forearms ache immediately from the recoil. Yet the man stands straight and unharmed, blocking the doorway; he threatens the man with the gun, then gestures for him to get out of the way. But then the stranger moves too fast, grabbing the barrel, yanking it away.

'Fuck, please no don't,' he begs.

'Lucy,' the man announces, and there is a wild grief in his eyes, the image of a man captured by a deep and total love, rising over a mountain ridge and coming to know the worst truth: a man dressed as his dead lover, a child drowned in a swimming pool, a massacred family wedding, a love lost to the mechanics of a cruel and unjust world. The man brings the gun to his own temple, and then his face and head is gone, swallowed by a torrent of noise, of blood, skin, hair, his body crumpling.

'Fuck oh fuck the fuck.'

Blindly, he is sprinting, smashing between walls, left, right, left, and nothing changes: each door is an equal unit of measurement apart and identical, no matter which direction he goes. He runs to the end of the hallway, right, into the stairwell, thudding footsteps on concrete, two at a time, then slamming through the door, crashing wildly. He scrambles forward, tripping slightly and dragging himself upright, right, left, stopping momentarily until he thinks he can hear that faint lobby music again, a tinkling that seems slightly sped up, and runs toward it. He nearly hits the front desk as he releases into the room; the music is now thunderous, a sonic blockade moving from piano into full orchestral, swelling as he pushes through the glass doors, wiggling through the chained gates, and then east, across Jarvis. He hears the steady pack of his running steps and can't control the whip of his head flinging behind him to see who is following; no one is pursuing him but still he sprints, past the tall black metal fence around a parking lot, the *Toronto Star* newspaper box beside him, open and spilling into the street and across his sidewalk path, the print grabbing his ankles, slipping around him.

Without slowing, he turns north, Mutual Street, crossing at an angle, around a city garbage bin, wood planks stacked neatly beside it, one side coloured sky blue and the other side dark with rot, nails protruding. To his left is a fenced-in area, multiple-function grey temporary trailers in a horseshoe, all movement absent except a large orange tarp covering a misshapen blob, a large animal sunk down to its knees in the centre of the trailer configuration, the breeze making it heave like lungs. He sprints alongside tidy blue barrels, unmarked, with scrubby grass growing around them, tipped with canary-coloured flowers, and then he leans left down Frank Natale Lane.

To his right is a small enclave, tiled a grimy beige, and two doors; *Transformer Vault Room Do Not Block*, he reads as he rests, hands on his knees. He can hear heavy machinery grinding, then the boom of a jet overhead. But there are no human noises, no voices or footsteps, no one: he peers back the way he came and Dundas Street is vacant, still, trash blowing serenely between the streetcar tracks and abandoned cars. His foot is shocked by stepping into a shallow puddle, strewn with disintegrating wrappers, a red-and-green ribbon, and fruit peels from the row of compost bins that have been toppled, slippery and putrid. He sees a message on the wall, *We poison the air and your body*, and there are signs declaring that the area is under surveillance, the bubbled camera staring back at him from the corners. He can see himself in the reflection of the camera and is surprised by how strong he looks. *I can make it*, he thinks, *I can't go back now.*

Reaching into his pocket, he feels the jagged snags of his broken phone screen before he sees them, but is relieved when he presses the power button and the screen lights up. There are no messages and his phone still reads no reception. He imagines Melanie at her kitchen table, checking her phone repeatedly too, refreshing social media, scared by his silence. As he is returning the phone, there is the rapid fire of automatic gunfire, popping viciously from the direction he just fled. A flash in his mind: the gun, the stranger's eyes squeezed close in relief, his father's cancer-rotted weary smile, then the eruption. He hitches, his tensed inhales buckling his chest tight.

His eyes adjust from the dark in a squint as he leaves into the sunlight, fighting the urge to run across Dalhousie Street, toward the gas station at the corner of Church and Dundas. Instead, he calmly turns the corner of the building, faces a Tim Hortons and Circle K and a hastily spray-painted pink cross on the ground that has faded into the dry weeds. He moves over the concrete parking stall markers, between yellow stripes, slipping sideways between the cars; he is forced to shift, labyrinthine, between the haphazard vehicles, each slanted, and then left around the pumps, glinting and quiet.

He refuses to let the voice from the Conservatory bathroom or the face of the stranger with the gun to his temple invade, and instead focuses on the smell of gas that lingers among the discarded vehicles, washing over and reminding him of his family road trips across BC. They were brief six-hour excursions down two-lane twists, the thin trunks of spruce and pine in the altitudes, density, layers upon layers that would crawl up the mountains, his father staring straight ahead, gripping the wheel, and his mother with her hand on his knee, changing the radio station when the static overtook the voices and music; during these drives, he would take great care not to make a noise, to look out the window and be invisible, until they pulled into a gas station and his mother would let him buy one thing, a bag of chips or a fistful of five-cent candy, and his father would get a stubby coffee. The sun would set on their way home, and they would descend into the flat valley bottom, horses scattered behind sagging fencing in tall summer grass, the sedimentary hues would bleed across the horizon, make shadows of everything until the dark overtook it all.

He surfaces from that calm and safety back into the city, into the traffic and the streetcar stop at Dundas and Church. He is alone underneath the lacework of cables overhead at the intersection, zagging in all directions, south past the gaudy oranges of the Pizza Pizza; spinning, he sees the horizon empty in all directions, until he sees the spire of a southward church and the cloud, thick and midnight, gobbling the cross from the top. Across Dundas, the Bond Place Hotel rises, and he cranes his neck, the tower lifting impossibly into the sky, the windows covered sporadically with sheer curtains and vertical blinds, the occasional unreadable face glooming down on him, then pulling back into its room. There is a curve in the street in front of him, as Dundas pushes toward Yonge, and he brushes by the Burrito Brothers, then a pawn shop, a blank storefront with paper blocking the view in, then another copy shop next to the Imperial Pub. He stops, hears the diesel cough of something large south of him, then squawking radios in cacophony, the drag of metal on asphalt, boots stomping, irregular signs of distressed movements en masse, an unnerving system rotating and churning into its places and stations. Then there is the burst of airplanes: looking skyward he sees a triangle of pointed jets zoom over his head and west.

He creeps up to the entrance of the pub, cautious of being seen. There is a clatter, then a swarm of engines, and he freezes until he is certain he hears no one approaching, and feels his phone vibrate against his leg. He hugs along the wall until he reaches its doorway, where he is offset from the street and out of view. He shelters himself while reaching for his phone, reading a system alert from the province: *There has been an incident in the downtown core of Toronto that has released dangerous airborne agents. Please stay indoors until further notifications. Further information to come.* He taps to his conversation with Melanie and sees that she has read his last message, but there is no reply. Suddenly, he remembers that they had spent time at this bar. Before they were together, he had spent nights there sitting at the circular bar that centred the downstairs room, dark wood everywhere, watching baseball or football or whatever was on the TV, and drinking whatever beer was on special, filling his head with fuzz, the occasional sexual fantasy, foam. On their date, he had met her outside, guided her in and to his usual spot at the bar; she ordered house wine, and the bartender served them by asking her how she knew him.

'Oh, we're seeing each other. I wanted to see where he hung out.'

'This place? Everyone in here knows him.'

Swigging, he smiled, made some joke about being a dedicated alcoholic, and later, after talking, they had kissed outside, him pressing her against the pillar just outside the door, her tongue swirling excitedly in his mouth. The memory overtakes him: they catch a cab back to her place that night and go right to her bed, throwing the oversized pillows to the floor, pulling the covers back; he lies on his back, naked, and watches her pull her T-shirt over her head, wiggling out of her jeans; he masturbates slowly as she pulls down her panties, climbs in beside him; this vision meshes with a memory of her body curving by the moonlight, their mouths on each other, and her rapid breathing timed to his thrusting, her body curling to his with her neck thrown back, that arch of tendons and muscles.

She saw his text but was interrupted before she could answer it, he convinces himself. She needs him. But the memory of their sex collides with those of the hunting knife, the sabre, the hotel voices and gunshot, the couple yelling on the sidewalk, the birds swirling into skulls, her door closing and sending him into the night, the cloud storming north overtop the whole city; it all blends into one furious substance, inseparable, and it engulfs him with a savage wave, rooting him to the spot.

Then, suddenly, a large explosion roars close enough to rattle his chest, the windows; this is immediately followed by a smaller shudder that he feels through his feet, calves. He tries the door closest to him first, finds it locked, and jogs past the large dark windows to the second door, which also doesn't move when he pushes his weight against it. He moves back toward the first door, pauses, and cups his hands to look in: the cheap wooden chairs are disarrayed, one of the round tables on its side, a smashed bottle with its liquor entrails trailing down to the linoleum. There is a flash, and movement near the back; the rectangle of a phone lights up, female facial features briefly carved from the dark before winking out. He knocks then, first tentatively, then harder, and then the phone flicks on again before a third detonation ravages his organs with a swell of corkscrew vibrations, assaulting and pillaging him. He uses both hands to slap the glass, checking behind him, until he sees a ghostly shimmer, a body under moonlight: the face is clear and contorted in mock-orgasmic pleasure, arching neck and mouth open in a wide O, before it recedes back into the dark. 'Let me in! Please!' he yells, but any presence has faded away completely. He tries the first door, then the second, peering back in, rattling the handles, hitting the glass.

Finally, his breath deepens, lengthens, as his muscles slacken slightly, just enough for him to move away from the pub, knowing there is only one direction he can go: he can't return, he is too far along, and so he moves west, between the rows of rental bike racks to his left, moving lightly around them, and along a former eyeglasses store now with the window boarded over, along the north side of Dundas Street, approaching Victoria Street, the edge of Yonge-Dundas Square. *West.*

The space is marked by an orgy of advertisements, electronic billboards, cosmetic signage for stores, and the jumble of office buildings surrounding the flat plaza across the street. Giant faces smile benignly, laughing, shifting between movie trailers and stores in clashing fonts, *Jack Astor's, Dollarama, GoodLife Fitness.* Under these gazes, the square has been transformed and the usual foot traffic has been replaced by soldiers in military green, gleaming rifles. Opposite him, there are wooden barricades keeping any traffic from going south down Victoria, and a garbage truck parked perpendicular that blocks any view; he can see a group of army fatigues gathered, can hear the radios jabbering as they talk in a circle, not noticing him as they adjust their rifles from shoulder to shoulder. The heat of the afternoon is bearing down on them, the sweat gathering in their uniforms at their armpits and the backs of their knees. He can feel the agitation and high alert as he slinks slowly, slightly north, up Victoria and then across, in front of Freedom Mobile, Blaze Pizza; he can see the contours of jeeps parked in the square, a large green transport truck, and, warily, he goes past the entrance to the subway, the dormant Starbucks. It is only then that he notices the military helicopter hovering at the edges of the thick plume of downtown smoke that is blooming out over the entire city; the first helicopter is joined by a second, farther west, and it flies along the expanse of the cloud. He crosses the street so that he can move unseen along the barricades, and under the cover of the rotors and sirens, he is momentarily ignored by the soldiers with their backs to him. When he emerges from behind the tall barriers blocking his view, he is startled by the two massive tanks that have been parked facing each other, their treads resting, sinking into the pavement outside the H&M and Eaton Centre, the barrels of their guns swung so that they almost cross, pointing opposite each other. Behind the hulking machines, Yonge Street slips southward toward the lake.

'You can't go this way. You need to get indoors.' The sheen and tint of the tanks' metal attacks him, catching the sun at certain angles and redirecting it into his eyes. Despite the glare, he can see that the soldier yelling at him is wearing a gas mask.

Somehow, he can hear him clearly: 'Go north. Follow Yonge. You cannot go any further. Get indoors. Now. You can't be here. You need to go. Now.'

Beyond the barking voice, he sees her: Melanie is struggling to get away from two soldiers on either side of her who have her by the elbows, their grip biting violently into the blue of her long dress; her mouth is wide in a scream but there is no noise as the two drag her backward and away from him, her heels along the pavement and over the curb. *Another, what, is it really her?* The man on the left leers at him, then raises his hand to her breast and squeezes grotesquely as she whips her body back and forth, her limbs wild and flailing against the olive-green fatigues, before the trio is out of view, around the corner of a flimsy temporary building.

He bolts forward, ducking under a tank barrel, and is running in their direction.

'Stop! Stop!' There is a new man whose pistol is drawn and trained on his body, causing him to pull up in a skid. Dust swirls around the man's ankles as he holds the gun steady on him, the sun high and crushing down on the two; they are the only figures in the barren silent stretch of Yonge Street, a paper napkin blowing between them in lazy cycles. 'Stop.' Watching the sheen of the man's gun barrel, he drops his own arms to his side, eyeing the corner of the building where they took her, then the man directly in his path. The gun follows this movement, and the man's eyes track the same path as his. They are opposite, legs wide.

'Where are they taking her?' he demands.

'Her?'

'I just saw them. Where are they taking her?' He begins to slowly move his hands to his waistband.

The soldier twitches, and his expression hardens as he understands, his glare sharpening into a squint, hand drifting to his sidearm.

He reaches for the empty place where his gun used to be.

There is a loud sharp noise, then a continuous and powerful darkness imposing on him, pouring over him like a thunderhead along a valley, total and raging and beyond human control; the darkness is thick as pitch and widens around him as he descends, lowering into the formless widening advance of black, the smell of cut grass and bleach and pepper and fish rot. When he looks upward he sees the same endless expanse of shadow, and he feels heat licking at his body but sees no flame, no light or flicker, only the enveloping fever around him that covers him like the smoke of a wildfire, forests burning and the atmosphere filled with the predatory teeth of a void, the hollow blank of a freshly dug grave in wet, fresh soil. He moves downward until shapes start to emerge: first, they are wisps of movement, breath or wind, generating waves back and forth as if sand drawn back and forth by tides, and the shapes start to slowly solidify into fields, stretches of corn running infinitely in every direction, their tall forms blowing gently, and he knows he is close to his parents' home, a length of land that the nearby ranch uses to grow feed for their cattle; he knows it's early spring because he can hear calving in the distance, low moans from just beyond the fences that hold the ocean of cow corn, sharp leaves, husks and chaff surrounding him. This shifts, and the stalks join, thicken into trunks, branches, woods, and he is at the lake's edge with his father, the water unbroken except for the red-and-white spheres of plastic bobbing and signalling where their lures are sunk. A loon calls somewhere and his father is telling him a story about being young: 'He was a fucking bastard,' he insists,

'God, I hated him for such a long time,' and he nods as his father continues, 'And I thought when you were born, your mother and I thought, I could change things, things might be different for you, they had to be,' and the rod jerks quickly then settles, 'But fuck, I'm the same, I can see it and feel it,' and his voice evens out, 'I've taught you a lot, though, I'm happy with that. I taught you all the things I know.' His father is dying, and this is one of the last times the two can climb through the forest and follow the slope to the curled and sheltered bay they always fish from. 'He used to take me out, out of the house, so my mother wouldn't hear the whole of it,' he pauses, tracking along the opposite shore, 'She knew, but I don't think she knew he would take me to the barn, to this flat space, it was sort of a circle. They had machines that did it back then, for the grain, but before, when he was young and his father would take him there, he always called that part of the barn the threshing floor.' His father coughs, one hand falling to his knee, but hitches forward with his speech, 'He said that's where the good grain could be separated,' and only then does he notice the wire extending from his father's wrist and the machine attached, monitoring his vitals with lines and numbers, the oxygen tube running into his nostrils, into his throat and lungs and circulating through his father's giant body. The contrast of the hospital equipment and the lake startles him, and his father calls his name as he backs cautiously away, and he calls his name again as he turns to run into the woods, his father swaggering after him with crashing steps, now lazily pulling the vowels of his name as he drawls; he blindly follows a packed-down trail through the woods and doesn't stop running until he is out of breath, pressed against the trunk of a fir, hard sap under his fingers and the tickling branches on his wrists, the air lurching from his lungs. When

he regains enough of himself, he pushes away from the bark
and turns and sees the young boy: he is stark against the grove
and holding his own head in the crook of his arm, his neck
vacant and oozing blood, and the boy's mouth moves and his
voice sounds like a body thrashing in water. He spins to flee and
he trips over a root, falling onto all fours on the smooth ground;
the ground is paved and his palms are grinding into the stray
grain that is scattered underneath him, the kernels pressing into
the grooves of his hands. He raises his head, and his father is
reaching out his hand to him, pulling him to his feet: they are in
his childhood's local mall, walking past a cellphone store, the
lotto kiosk, a suit rental shop, familiar facades and colours,
generic and unchanged over decades, a nonplace, and his father
strides purposefully forward, his boots echoing on the hard
floor in horse-hoof clips, just outside arm's length; he admires
the simultaneous grace and power in that walk, balance and
dexterity, determination. Then his father takes one last step and
collapses, crumpling under the harsh fluorescent lights, dust
springing up around him. 'I'll get help!' he shouts to his prone
father, and begins to spring toward the food court, desperate,
retching, turning the corner to his high school cafeteria; it is
completely upheaved, and teenagers are running by him, one
missing an arm, another holding a bloody face, away from the
smouldering centre, away from the blackened and warped plastic
chairs and overturned tables, scorched and melted. There is
smoke coursing out from the hole in the tiled floor, coal and
smothering and darkly expanding, accompanied by a thrum-
ming drone, guttural, deep underneath his feet and through his
legs; he is paralyzed in place, despite the close-by rake of automatic gunfire, looking at the devastation, a witness to this vista
of destruction, and the smoke churns into the images of

annihilated badlands, burning homesteads, demolished war camps, tracts of desert with a horizon as long and far as human vision. The landscape rises up in a tsunami above him, a massive wave of sand that rushes at him, and he goes limp, accepting, shuts his eyes; he feels himself completely covered, immobile, the silt is in each pore, every crease of skin, and he can feel it leaking into his ears, intruding upon his eye sockets and lips. The swell continues, the sounds of its cresting and flooding now high above him as he is buried deeper and deeper under the pressure of its crush, lightless, the surface now distant, muffled. He remains in that blackness until he notices sounds rising around him, the grind of cranes into buildings, sirens, a calf's bleat, the shouts of men in pursuit, snow falling in an empty marsh, a voice: she is in conversation, not quite audible, it is Melanie's voice, it is his mother's voice, it is whispering and drifting between the jangle of a pay phone's ring, a family speaking Japanese, this collection whirling around his father's pale and weak voice. When he does finally open his eyes, he is in the dim light of a hotel room, a neon sign lightly painting the pane of the window in bright green, and all sound drops away, and he is abandoned in the middle of its worn carpet, the centre of the room. There is a burble from the corner and he slowly pivots to its source. He is faced with a slumped body, a gun pressed against what was once its temple, the spread of the skull behind on the wall and dripping, his hand gripping a snatch of a dress's fabric. It falls from the body's hand and the fabric's clean white reflects the light through the window, and the room changes one final time: he is lit by the flicker of a late-night movie on the hospital TV, the rhythmic sounds of the ventilator expanding and contracting his father's lungs, as he lies in the bed, the sheet pulled up to his chin; he traces the outline of his diminished father underneath, a casing, a breathing ghost. He stands by the edge of the bed, waiting as he waited before, his father dying as he did before, and his helpless body becomes a silhouette receding into the darkness, into a barren boundary, into wild, flat, empty space.

And then the dark door closes.

ACKNOWLEDGEMENTS

I have been very fortunate to have been supported in a myriad of ways while writing this book, and I owe many debts of gratitude.

To Alana Wilcox for your incredible insights and editing. To James Lindsay for reading so closely and guiding this book with such intelligence. To the rest of the Coach House team, for being nothing but a joy to work with. To Ingrid Paulson for the cover that pulls it all together. To Stuart Ross for always reading carefully.

To Emily Schultz, John Haskell, and Naben Ruthnum for your generosity, and for being terrific inspirations.

To Derek Beaulieu and the Banff Centre for Arts and Creativity, where I was given the time and space to flesh out this book in my little boat in the woods.

To the Ontario Arts Council, Toronto Arts Council, and Canada Council for the Arts for providing stability and headspace to get this book all the way to the finish line.

To all of you who read this book at various stages and showed kindness to its raggedness (in no particular order): Brian Dedora, Aaron Peck, Cody Caetano, Ralph Kolewe, and Stephen Murphy. To everyone else who talked with me about the book over coffee and/or beers, who asked and chatted in the middle of a global pandemic, and were so nourishing. There are too many to list, but I will thank you all individually in some way, I promise.

To my mom and dad, who have always allowed me to be as I am, despite myself.

To Julia Polyck-O'Neill, my total and complete love.

Aaron Tucker is the author of the novel *Y: Oppenheimer, Horseman of Los Alamos* (Coach House Books); three books of poetry: *Catalogue d'oiseaux* (Book*hug Press), *Irresponsible Mediums: The Chess Games of Marcel Duchamp* (Book*hug Press), and *punchlines* (Mansfield Press); and two scholarly cinema studies monographs, *Virtual Weaponry: The Militarized Internet in Hollywood War Films* and *Interfacing with the Internet in Popular Cinema* (both published by Palgrave Macmillan).

He is currently a PhD candidate in the Cinema and Media Studies Department at York University, where he is studying the cinema of facial recognition software and its impacts on citizenship, mobility, and crisis.

Typeset in Albertina and Baskerville 10.

Printed at the Coach House on bpNichol Lane in Toronto, Ontario, on Zephyr Antique Laid paper, which was manufactured, acid-free, in Saint-Jérôme, Quebec, from second-growth forests. This book was printed with vegetable-based ink on a 1973 Heidelberg KORD offset litho press. Its pages were folded on a Baum-folder, gathered by hand, bound on a Sulby Auto-Minabinda, and trimmed on a Polar single-knife cutter.

Coach House is on the traditional territory of many nations, including the Mississaugas of the Credit, the Anishnabeg, the Chippewa, the Haudenosaunee, and the Wendat peoples, and is now home to many diverse First Nations, Inuit, and Métis peoples. We acknowledge that Toronto is covered by Treaty 13 with the Mississaugas of the Credit. We are grateful to live and work on this land.

Edited by James Lindsay and Alana Wilcox
Cover design by Ingrid Paulson
Interior design by Crystal Sikma
Author photo by Julia Polyck-O'Neill

Coach House Books
80 bpNichol Lane
Toronto ON M5S 3J4
Canada

416 979 2217
800 367 6360

mail@chbooks.com
www.chbooks.com